MUSIC TO GET KILLED BY

"This is the building," Frank whispered when he and Joe reached the warehouse. "There doesn't seem to be anybody here."

"What if this is a trap?" Joe replied.

"We're about to find out," Frank said, trying a side door. It opened easily, and they stepped inside.

The warehouse was a two-story expanse with a balcony covering half the first floor. Forklifts and handtrucks were positioned among thousands of boxes and crates.

Joe began poking into a couple of boxes. "These are full of CDs," he announced. "Looks like we've found a major part of the operation."

Just then Frank heard a sound. He glanced up quickly to the balcony. A heavy crate had been launched over the railing and was plummeting straight toward Joe!

Books in THE HARDY BOYS CASEFILES® Series

#1 DEAD ON TARGET
#2 EVIL, INC.
#3 CULT OF CRIME
#4 THE LAZARUS PLOT
#5 EDGE OF DESTRUCTION
#6 THE CROWNING TERROR
#7 DEATHGAME
#8 SEE NO EVIL
#9 THE GENIUS THIEVES
#10 HOSTAGES OF HATE
#11 BROTHER AGAINST BROTHER
#12 PERFECT GETAWAY
#13 THE BORGIA DAGGER
#14 TOO MANY TRAITORS
#15 BLOOD RELATIONS
#16 LINE OF FIRE
#17 THE NUMBER FILE
#18 A KILLING IN THE MARKET
#19 NIGHTMARE IN ANGEL CITY
#20 WITNESS TO MURDER
#21 STREET SPIES
#22 DOUBLE EXPOSURE
#23 DISASTER FOR HIRE
#24 SCENE OF THE CRIME
#25 THE BORDERLINE CASE
#26 TROUBLE IN THE PIPELINE
#27 NOWHERE TO RUN
#28 COUNTDOWN TO TERROR
#29 THICK AS THIEVES
#30 THE DEADLIEST DARE
#31 WITHOUT A TRACE
#32 BLOOD MONEY
#33 COLLISION COURSE
#34 FINAL CUT
#35 THE DEAD SEASON
#36 RUNNING ON EMPTY
#37 DANGER ZONE
#38 DIPLOMATIC DECEIT
#39 FLESH AND BLOOD
#40 FRIGHT WAVE
#41 HIGHWAY ROBBERY
#42 THE LAST LAUGH
#43 STRATEGIC MOVES
#44 CASTLE FEAR
#45 IN SELF-DEFENSE
#46 FOUL PLAY
#47 FLIGHT INTO DANGER
#48 ROCK 'N' REVENGE
#49 DIRTY DEEDS
#50 POWER PLAY
#51 CHOKE HOLD
#52 UNCIVIL WAR
#53 WEB OF HORROR
#54 DEEP TROUBLE
#55 BEYOND THE LAW
#56 HEIGHT OF DANGER
#57 TERROR ON TRACK
#58 SPIKED!
#59 OPEN SEASON
#60 DEADFALL
#61 GRAVE DANGER
#62 FINAL GAMBIT
#63 COLD SWEAT
#64 ENDANGERED SPECIES
#65 NO MERCY
#66 THE PHOENIX EQUATION
#67 LETHAL CARGO
#68 ROUGH RIDING
#69 MAYHEM IN MOTION
#70 RIGGED FOR REVENGE
#71 REAL HORROR
#72 SCREAMERS
#73 BAD RAP

Available from ARCHWAY Paperbacks

BAD RAP

FRANKLIN W. DIXON

AN ARCHWAY PAPERBACK
Published by POCKET BOOKS
New York London Toronto Sydney Tokyo Singapore

This book is a work of fiction. Names, characters, places and incidents are either the product of the author's imagination or are used fictitiously. Any resemblance to actual events or locales or persons, living or dead, is entirely coincidental.

AN ARCHWAY PAPERBACK *Original*

An Archway Paperback published by
POCKET BOOKS, a division of Simon & Schuster Inc.
1230 Avenue of the Americas, New York, NY 10020

Produced by Mega-Books of New York, Inc.

ISBN: 0-671-73109-2

First Archway Paperback printing March 1993

10 9 8 7 6 5 4 3 2 1

Cover art by Brian Kotzky

Printed in the U.S.A.

IL 6+

BAD RAP

Chapter 1

"EARTH TO JOE!" Frank Hardy exclaimed. "Watch where you're going!"

Frank grabbed his brother, Joe, by the shoulder to keep him from walking right into a pile of boxes stacked in the corner of the rehearsal studio.

"If I'd known you were going to get all star-struck," Frank said, "I'd have left you at home."

Joe hadn't heard a word his brother said. Even though he couldn't hear what was happening in the glass-enclosed rehearsal space in front of them, his attention was riveted on it. Hip-hop star Randy Rand was inside, practicing with his group, the Power Brokers. Rand was Joe's latest idol, and the younger Hardy had talked about nothing else the whole way into New York City from Bayport, where the Hardys lived.

The only time Joe took his eyes off Rand was to smile at Tabitha Cowan, who was standing on his right. Tabitha was president of Tight Fist Records, Rand's label. With her long blond hair and bright blue eyes, Tabitha resembled a model more than a recording tycoon. She was young, too—not much older than Frank or Joe.

Tabitha watched with the Hardys as Rand finished up. She then excused herself and headed into the booth.

"I still can't believe Randy Rand called us to help him," Joe said.

"I can't wait to find out what he needs help with," Frank said.

"All we know is that he has a problem," Joe confirmed, smiling at the booth where Tabitha was. "If it gives me a chance to hang out with him—and her—I'm all for it."

Frank grinned ruefully. Joe had a tendency sometimes to get too involved with the people in their cases. It seemed to Frank that now was going to be one of those times. Since he was the older and more serious of the two, it was usually up to him to keep Joe focused on the case.

Since they had solved their first mystery, Frank and Joe Hardy had earned quite a good reputation as amateur detectives. Sometimes their father, Fenton Hardy, a former police officer and now an internationally known private investigator, sent a case or two their way. This time, though, Randy Rand and Tabitha Cowan had heard about them and called them directly to ask them to come to New York City. Since it was June and school was out, the Hardys had jumped at the chance. Neither of them knew what the case was about, and Frank was itching to get to work.

In the booth Randy was toweling off his bare chest. The rap star wore extra baggy pants and hightops. Several gold chains hung around his neck, and he wore three gold earrings in his left ear. With his babyish face, Rand didn't look much older than Joe.

Randy and the other two men in the booth began to pack up the synthesizer and drum set.

"Well, we're about to find out why rap star extraordinaire Randy Rand sent for us," Joe said, motioning toward Tabitha and Randy, who were approaching them.

"Randy," Tabitha announced, "this is Frank and Joe Hardy."

"Awesome!" Randy exclaimed, slapping first Frank's hand and then Joe's. "These are the dudes that are going to get me a little justice."

"Your music is really def," Joe replied. "I have your new CD. 'What U Do' is my favorite track."

"Thanks, man," Randy said. "Hey, I want

you two to meet my boys, the Power Brokers." He pointed to the two men who were packing up the equipment in the booth. "That's Tony and Dr. D."

Tony and Dr. D were about nineteen, Frank thought. Tony had long black hair pulled back into a ponytail. He was bare-chested and was wearing jeans. Dr. D, a muscular young black man, wore bright yellow shorts, a black-and-yellow shirt, and a yellow baseball cap snugged on backward.

Checking out his own button-down shirt and khaki pants, Frank felt a little out of place.

"They're fresh," Frank said. "Maybe we should get down to it, though, and you should explain to us why you called."

"Mr. Business," Randy said, taking in Frank. "I like it. Well, check this. I'm a poor kid from Brooklyn who hooks up with the baddest jammies in the world, right. We take hip-hop by storm, and then one day I notice these dupes—duplicates, in case you don't know—of my tapes and CDs popping up all over Chinatown. Unauthorized copies. Bottom line: Randy's getting ripped."

"We went to the police," Tabitha put in, her arms folded across her chest. "They're working on it, but they said their caseload was too full for them to investigate fully. They said the FBI usually handles cases like this, but the Bureau doesn't have time, either. Too busy."

Randy shook his head and made a face. "Tell me about it. Then I remembered reading about you dudes in the paper. Since nobody else can help us, I thought you could. That's why I had Tabitha call you."

"So our job is to find out who's counterfeiting the CDs and turn them over to the police," Frank replied.

"Before Tight Fist Records goes broke," Tabitha added with a sigh. "The dupes on the street are selling better than our own stock. This sort of scam could break us. The peddlers are setting up racks on the streets and selling the copies for a lot less than a reputable store would. The counterfeits are so good that people don't realize they're getting ripped off."

"I don't understand," said Joe. "Why can't the police bust the vendors?"

"Hey, dude—you know how many street vendors there are in Chinatown, not to mention New York City?" Randy said.

"Besides, some of the street merchants have been caught. The most the police could do was recover the dupes and fine them," Tabitha said. "The counterfeiter is the one we've got to find."

"That's right," Frank replied. "If we want to stop this, we have to find the distributor. You won't have to worry about the street vendors if we shut the counterfeiter down."

"I'm hip," Randy replied. "You happy with your room in the Gramercy Hotel?" The boys nodded. "I got some more work around here, but we can meet back there later tonight and make a plan."

Frank glanced at his watch. It was already eight P.M. They'd already spent too much time at the studio waiting around.

"I'd like to head over to Chinatown now and start sniffing around," Frank said. "It's possible that the operation is based there since that's where the vendors have been spotted. Illegal activities like this usually go down at night."

Randy grinned. "Mr. Business is on the ball." Dr. D motioned to Randy from inside the booth. "Look, I've got to get back to help. I'll check you two later."

Frank and Joe said goodbye to Tabitha and left the studio, stepping outside onto the crowded sidewalk of the East Village, a neighborhood in lower Manhattan. Frank wiped the sweat off his forehead. The city was hot and muggy, even at night.

Joe reached out to hail a cab. The brothers had decided it would be easier to leave their van back in Bayport and get around the city by subway, bus, and cab. An empty yellow taxi pulled up to the curb in front of them, and Frank and

Joe piled into the back. Frank pulled the door shut behind him and told the driver to take them to Chinatown. The Hardys had been to New York a lot and knew their way around.

The driver steered the cab into traffic, hitting a button to start the meter.

"Tabitha sure is gorgeous," Joe said, running his hands through his blond hair. "In fact, she has all the qualities I look for in a woman: beauty, power, wealth."

"Don't think years of hard work and determination have put her where she is," Frank told him. "I did a little research on Tight Fist Records before we left Bayport. Tabitha is from a pretty wealthy family. Her father, Doyle Cowan, earned a fortune in the entertainment field. He owns shares of a major movie studio, of recording labels, even of a string of cineplexes around the country. He bought Tight Fist for Tabitha. She's his only child, and I guess he wants to see if she can make a go of it and handle the responsibility."

"It looks like she can to me," Joe said. "She's a pro, don't you think?"

Frank shrugged. "Who knows. From what I found out, Tight Fist Records has had its share of financial problems. Randy Rand is the only breakaway star they've got. This counterfeit business could ruin them."

"I can imagine what she must be going through,"

Joe said in sympathy. "She's trying to prove to her dad that she has what it takes to be successful. She finally starts to make strides, then someone comes along and tries to sink her."

"Most record companies have to deal with this sort of thing," Frank replied. "But for a small label like Tight Fist, counterfeiters can be a disaster."

"Where do we start?" Joe asked as the cab pulled to a stop.

"Where we always start," Frank said, handing the driver a twenty. "At the bottom."

Joe got out of the cab while Frank waited for his change. On the crowded sidewalk, above the din of bustling crowds of shoppers, Frank could make out someone playing Randy's song "What U Do."

"What you do / I do too / get past the skin / I'm just like you / I breathe the air / the earth we share / we should unite / and fight for right . . ."

"That's what I like about Randy's music," Joe said to Frank. "He has a real social conscience."

"Right," Frank replied, plunging into the crowd.

Street vendors jammed the sidewalks, while merchants stood in open storefronts. Frank and Joe worked their way through the throng. Frank saw fish, vegetables, stereo equipment, and jewelry all prominently displayed side by side for passersby.

Joe grabbed his brother's arm. "Check it out," he said. "Randy's tapes and CDs are everywhere, along with ones by other popular groups. No wonder Tabitha wants this business to stop."

"There are probably thousands of dupes here," Frank agreed. "And every single person who buys one is undercutting Tight Fist's profits. What a rip-off!"

Frank paused as a kid, barely twelve, tugged on his sleeve. "You want to buy some tapes, mister?" The kid was dressed in faded jeans and a light blue T-shirt. A red bandanna covered his head.

Frank examined the tapes the kid was holding out to them. Randy's were among them. "No," Frank said, a plan formulating in his mind. "But I do have a business proposition for you."

"What kind of proposition?" the kid asked suspiciously.

"We work for someone who's interested in buying into a business," Frank said. "I notice your tapes are missing bar codes and copyright information."

"What are you talking about?" the kid asked. "These are legit."

"Calm down," Frank said reassuringly. "Our boss is interested in making an investment, that's all. If you could give us a little information, turn us on to the right people, my boss would cut you in on the action."

"Are you guys cops?" the kid demanded.

"Do we look like cops?" Joe replied.

"No!" the kid exclaimed, pointing a finger at Joe. "But if you're not cops, then tell me you're not. I heard cops can't lie about being cops."

"We're not cops," Joe retorted.

"Okay then," the kid said, grinning. "If you're telling the truth, then tell your boss my name is Billy Nguyen. If you're lying, then you never heard of me. Either way, you'll have to buy every one of these cassettes before I give you an address. Deal?"

"Deal," Frank replied with a smile.

"One hundred dollars for ten cassettes!" Joe exclaimed as he and Frank made their way down a deserted street on the west side of Manhattan that was lined with warehouses. "I can't believe you let that kid soak you."

"Billy may have saved us hours of legwork," Frank insisted. "Besides, I want to check out these tapes. We might find some evidence on them."

As Frank and Joe walked down the street to find the address the kid had given them, not even a car passed them. "This is the building," Frank whispered as they reached a dark warehouse. "There doesn't seem to be anybody here."

"What if this is a trap?" Joe replied in a hushed voice.

"We're about to find out," Frank said, trying a side door. It opened easily. They stepped into the barely lit warehouse. Frank felt along the wall, found a light switch, flipped it on, and called out a hello.

The warehouse was a two-story expanse with a balcony covering half the first floor. Forklifts and handtrucks were positioned among thousands of boxes and crates. Joe walked farther into the maze and began poking into a couple of boxes. Frank noticed that the crates were all marked Hong Kong.

"These are full of CDs," Joe announced. "Looks like we've found a major part of the operation."

Just then Frank heard a sound. He glanced up quickly to the balcony. A heavy crate had been launched over the railing and was plummeting straight toward Joe!

Chapter 2

"LOOK OUT!" Frank shouted.

The huge crate was falling fast. With a mere second between him and disaster, Joe dove and rolled out of harm's way.

The crate splintered apart the second it hit the concrete floor. Stacks of CDs went flying.

Joe lay sprawled on the concrete, staring at the mess, the blood pounding in his head. Adrenaline raced through him.

"I could have been killed!" he said to his brother.

Then Joe thought to look up at the second-floor balcony. A young man peered over the railing at him.

"Frank! Look! Someone pushed the crate!"

Joe shouted angrily. "He's still up there! Come on. He's not getting away."

Joe reached the stairs before Frank. Skipping every other step, he quickly ascended the stairs. When he reached the top, he didn't see anyone. Where had the guy disappeared to?

Joe paused, listening to footfalls echoing farther away. He sprinted down the long narrow hallway, following his assailant's back.

The guy wore a blue jacket with a huge blue snake plastered across the back. Joe sped up, trying to close the distance between himself and the suspect. Frank was running right behind him now.

More big crates crowded the corridor. Joe had to weave between the boxes, jumping over some to maintain his speed.

The suspect frantically began to pull boxes down behind him to try to slow the Hardys down. "It won't do you any good!" Joe shouted, jumping over a splintered crate. A plastic CD case crunched beneath his foot. Joe lost his footing for a second but quickly regained his balance and continued the chase.

Finally he got within reaching distance. He grabbed a handful of the guy's jacket and pulled the kid to the ground, locking his head into the curve of his elbow.

"Let me go!" the guy screeched, trying to squirm away from Joe. He had long, thin blond hair. He was tall and wiry, but Joe was strong enough to pin and hold him.

"What's your name?" Joe demanded.

"Andy," the guy panted.

"Okay, Andy," Frank added over Joe's shoulder. "He's going to let you up. We want information. If you try to run again, we'll catch you. Understand?"

"Yeah, yeah." Andy quickly squirmed to his feet and glared suspiciously at Frank and Joe. "I should be the one questioning you," he said. "You're the ones trespassing. What are you doing here, anyway?"

"We work for someone with a business proposition for the owner of this warehouse," Frank said. "Billy Nguyen sent us."

"Billy sent you here?" Andy asked, surprised. He narrowed his eyes and stuffed his hands into the pockets of his jeans. "Just like that? Without even checking you out?"

"He checked us out," Joe said. "Now, why don't you tell us how we can find the owner instead of giving us a hard time?"

Andy took a deep breath and stared stonily at Frank and Joe for a long minute. "The guy you want to see is Blue Lou Chang," he said finally. "He's not here now."

"What's the story with Blue Lou?" Joe asked, pointing to a nearby crate. "He sure seems to have cornered the independent CD market."

Andy stiffened. "Chang's an importer of fine art and goods," he said. "The CDs aren't really his."

For the first time Joe took a good look around the warehouse. Downstairs there was an entire wall lined with oriental rugs, and he could see blue-and-white Chinese vases sticking up out of open crates.

"You want to explain why you tried to deck me with a crate?" Joe asked.

"I was here alone working on a rush delivery," Andy said defensively. "How was I supposed to know who you guys are? Like I said before, you were trespassing."

Andy had a point, Joe realized. They'd have to start being a little nicer to him if they wanted him to trust them.

Frank must have been thinking the same thing, because he walked up to Andy and put his hand out for a shake. "Sorry about that, Andy," Frank said. "Our boss sent us here hoping to make a deal, and I guess we were a little overanxious. We should have waited till tomorrow, but we're bottom-line guys, and the bottom line is you've got a warehouse full of CDs that our boss wants to buy into. He operates out of Miami and is interested in expanding his business. He really wants to hop on this Randy Rand boat—the guy is so hot. How do we get in touch with your boss?"

Andy shook his head slowly. "It's not my boss you want then. Blue Lou runs the importing business and rents space to other wholesalers. You'll have to get in touch with Jack Martinelli. He's the guy with the tapes and CDs."

"Where do we find Martinelli?" Joe asked.

"He operates out of Queens. Go to Nell's Discount on Sixtieth Street. They'll tell you where to find him," Andy replied.

"Thanks for your time, Andy," Frank said.

As soon as they were out of Andy's earshot, Joe said, "You took a real risk back there."

"How so?" Frank asked.

"Just coming right out and telling Andy we were interested in the CDs." Joe shook his head and let out a deep breath. "That could have backfired big time."

Frank shrugged. "I guess you're right, but he went along, no questions asked."

"True enough." Joe thought for a moment. "So what do you think? Is Martinelli in charge? I'm not convinced Chang's clean."

"Me either," Frank agreed, crossing the street ahead of Joe. All those CD crates were marked Hong Kong, which is where most CDs are duped. Chang might not be doing the actual counterfeiting, but it sure looks like he's distributing."

"You're probably right. We should run a check on him," Joe agreed. He peered down the dark street. "That is, if we ever get out of this neighborhood. It doesn't look like we're going to find a cab here."

"That's what the subway's for," said Frank. "I think there's a station one block down."

Half an hour later Frank and Joe were sitting in a subway speeding under the streets of New York.

"Tomorrow we'll go to Queens and try to get dirt on Martinelli. If this tip pays off, we might be heading back to Bayport by tomorrow night," Frank said.

"What about Blue Lou Chang?" Joe asked.

"I'm hoping to get lucky with Martinelli," Frank said. "We can always corner Chang at his warehouse."

"What kind of trouble could Martinelli be looking at?" Joe asked.

"Unauthorized duplication is a felony. I don't know about jail time, but hopefully it should be enough to make him quit the racket."

"I hope so," Joe said. "Randy seems like a nice guy."

The subway began to slow down, and Frank rose. "Come on," he said. "This is our stop."

Frank led the way out of the station and back up to the street. They were only a few blocks from the Gramercy Hotel. Joe followed his brother into the lobby and up to the front desk. The expensive carpets and plush sofas made the hotel seem just right for a star like Randy Rand. Joe wearily stared up at the clock above the desk: 11:55 P.M. No wonder he felt exhausted.

"Let's check our messages," Frank suggested. He approached the young woman behind the desk, who told them there was a message from Randy to join him in Room 420.

Joe and Frank headed for an elevator, which they took to the fourth floor. Stepping into the quiet hallway, Joe followed the door numbers to Room 420. He lightly knocked on the door.

"Yo, it's open," came Randy's voice.

The hip-hop star was stretched out on a bed, wearing loose-fitting sweats. The room was huge, with two queen-size beds separated by a nightstand. A table and four chairs were set up in the far corner of the room. Against one wall were a huge entertainment center and lots of stereo equipment.

"What's up, dudes?" Randy asked, sitting up.

"We questioned a kid in Chinatown and followed a lead to a warehouse near the Hudson River," Joe said, getting right into it. "We got some info there, and tomorrow we're going to Queens to check out another lead on a guy who might be duping your stuff."

"Who's that?" Randy asked.

"A man by the name of Jack Martinelli,"

Frank said. "You know what, Joe? I just thought of something. We should go to the chief of police tomorrow."

"You mean Sam Peterson?" Joe asked.

Frank nodded. "Peterson is our father's former partner," he told Randy. "He should be willing to help us bust this guy."

"Coolness!" Randy exclaimed. "I'm glad I asked Tabitha to call you two. The sooner this business is over, the better."

"I don't want to sound too optimistic," Joe interjected, "but it might be over tomorrow. If things go according to plan."

Randy jumped up from the bed. "How can I thank you guys?" he said, beaming excitedly.

"Don't thank us yet," Frank said. "Thank us when Martinelli gets busted."

"Why don't you guys chill here for a while?" Randy offered. "I don't get to socialize much in my line of work."

"I don't know," Frank said, standing up and checking his watch.

"We'd love to hang out," Joe replied, elbowing Frank lightly in the ribs.

Joe smiled as his brother reluctantly took a seat in a big armchair. It wasn't every day a guy got a chance to chat casually with Randy Rand, of all people. Apparently Frank wasn't going to louse this up for him.

"I guess we can stick around for an hour or so," Frank said.

"Great. We'll watch some tube," Randy said, going over to the entertainment center to grab the TV remote. He was standing and flipping through the channels when there was a loud banging on the door.

Joe bolted up as the doorknob turned and the door flew open.

A huge man in a sleeveless leather vest and dark jeans stood menacingly in the doorway.

Suddenly he rushed forward, straight at Randy.

"Randy Rand!" he bellowed. "I'm going to teach you not to mess with me, you little punk."

Chapter 3

FRANK LEAPT UP from his chair, ready to step between the big man and Randy. Joe moved into position, too. Randy slid in front of Joe and Frank, extending his arms to hold them back.

"It's cool," the rap star said with a smirk. "This here weasel is Beastmaster J. His bark is worse than his bite."

"Man! Who's calling who a weasel?" Beastmaster J bellowed. His voice was loud and deep. "I just found out that Tabitha Cowan booked the Power Brokers for a show at Madison Square Garden on the same bill as me!"

"All's fair, Beasty," Randy replied smugly.

"What's going on here, Randy?" Frank asked. "Who is this guy?"

"I know you've heard of Beastmaster J, Frank," Joe interrupted. "I have all his CDs, remember? He's, like, the king of rap."

"Not like," Beastmaster J said, his arms folded across his broad chest. "Try—I am the King of Rap."

The name clicked for Frank just then. "Wait a second," Frank said. "Randy, don't you have a song out called 'Beastmaster Jerk'?"

The Beastmaster lunged for Randy again. "That's right. This *baby* thinks he knows more than the master."

"You're history, old man," Randy shot back. "Besides, I was just having some fun."

"I don't really care what you think of me, Rand," Beastmaster J continued, "but you've got a lot of nerve, playing the same show as me."

"You're bugging me, man," Randy sneered. "The Power Brokers and me, we've brought the jam to an art form. You're just a creaky old dinosaur."

"You'll pay for this, Rand," Beastmaster J said, pointing at Randy. "You keep messing with the beast, you might just get bit."

Frank sighed as Beastmaster J turned sharply and left the room. "Are you sure antagonizing a guy like that is the right thing to do?" Frank asked.

"He won't do anything," Randy maintained. "He just likes to sound off."

"If you say so," Joe said with a shrug. "Maybe you should be careful, anyway. He's got a fist big enough to match that voice of his."

Randy laughed and punched Joe on the shoulder. "You guys are all right." He pushed the power button on the remote to turn on the TV. "How about kicking back like we were going to?"

Frank stifled a yawn. "I'm pretty tired," he said. "Besides, I want to get an early start in the morning."

"That's cool," Randy agreed. "I guess Beastmaster J kind of threw a wet blanket on the evening, anyway."

"Catch you later," Joe said as they left Randy's room to head for their own.

"Randy's pretty down to earth for such a superstar," Joe said as he and Frank got ready for bed. "Letting us hang out with him and all. Maybe we should stick around New York after we solve the case."

Frank hopped into bed. "Maybe we should solve the case first," he warned his brother as he turned off the bedside light.

After a quick breakfast of fruit and muffins in the hotel dining room the next day, Frank and Joe took a bus to the main police station downtown. Frank had called earlier and made an appointment with Chief of Police Peterson.

A blond-haired officer at the front desk directed the Hardys to an elevator, informing them that Peterson was expecting them.

When Frank and Joe got off the elevator they told Peterson's secretary they were there.

Sam Peterson emerged from his office and smiled brightly at the Hardys. The police chief was a fiftyish man whose dark hair was turning a bit silver and whose chocolate brown eyes took in everything. He was a bit beefy but fit enough still to outrun many of the young officers on the force.

"Frank and Joe Hardy," Peterson said, heartily shaking their hands. "I haven't seen you boys in ages. Come on into my office."

Frank sat in one of the chairs across from Peterson's desk and Joe pulled up a chair to sit next to him.

"So, how's your dad?" Peterson asked, sitting on the edge of his desk.

"Fine," Frank replied. "He sends his best."

Peterson smiled. "When you called, you said you'd need my help." He spread his arms. "I'm here to give it. What do you need?"

"We got a call from rap star Randy Rand yesterday morning," Frank said. "Have you heard of him?"

"Are you kidding? Any man with teenage kids knows his music," Peterson replied, shaking his head and grinning ruefully.

"It looks like someone is counterfeiting his tapes and CDs and selling them below the regular price," Frank continued. "He's asked us to help him track down the counterfeiter."

"We went to Chinatown last night," Joe put in, "and were directed to a warehouse owned by Blue Lou Chang as a possible source for the tapes. We think this Chang might be distributing counterfeit tapes and other stuff, but we don't think he's counterfeiting them. One of Chang's employees dropped the name of Jack Martinelli. He said he worked in Queens someplace."

"Martinelli and Chang?" Peterson said, stepping around to the computer on his desk and punching the names into his keyboard. "We've had our suspicions about Blue Lou Chang. The guy is a mob type. For income tax purposes he's an importer, but we know he has his fingers in everything. Surrounds himself with a youth gang as an army. Of course, we've never been able to pin anything on him."

Peterson put on a pair of reading glasses and stared at the screen. Silently he punched a few more keys and grunted.

"Martinelli, on the other hand, is a small-time hood," Peterson said. "He has a rap sheet a mile long. They're mostly minor offenses. Con jobs. Petty larceny. Blue Lou is a pretty tough customer, though, from what I understand. It would be odd for Martinelli to associate with a rough player like Chang."

"Do you think there could be a connection?" Joe asked.

"I don't know," Peterson said. "Chang is supposedly an importer. We've also had reports that Martinelli may be actually dubbing tapes in Queens and importing CDs from Hong Kong. Some of my men are already on the case."

Peterson hit a button on his phone. "Send Detective Torres in here, please."

A few minutes later, a stocky, dark-haired man wearing a white shirt, blue jacket, and red tie walked in.

"Frank and Joe Hardy, this is Pedro Torres," Peterson said. "Detective, I know these boys' father from way back. They seem to agree with what you've found out about Jack Martinelli. What's going on with your investigation?"

Torres eyed the boys suspiciously. "We just got a warrant to check out Martinelli's business, a warehouse in Queens," he said slowly. "We're about to go over there now."

Peterson stood up. "Do me a favor. Take Frank and Joe with you. I've worked with them before. They won't get in the way, I promise," he said with his eyes leveled at Joe.

"Whatever you say, Chief," Torres said.

Peterson turned to Frank to make his point stronger. "Keep an eye on that hot-headed brother of yours. See that you don't get into any trouble."

"Don't worry about us, sir," Frank said.

"Thanks," Joe added.

Frank and Joe followed Torres to the elevator. The detective took off ahead of them at a brisk pace.

"I want the two of you to know I'm not planning on being your baby-sitter," Torres said as they stepped onto the elevator. "How are you guys mixed up in this, anyway?"

"We're working for Randy Rand," Joe said.

Torres brightened. "*The* Randy Rand? No way. He's the best. Are you scamming me?"

"Nope," Frank said with a smile.

Torres became quiet and thoughtful. "I'll make you guys a deal. Get me a Randy Rand autograph and I'll let you hang out with me. Okay?"

"Okay!" Joe said quickly.

"Wait here," Torres said after they got off the elevator on the first floor.

After about ten minutes he returned with a man and a woman who Frank guessed were also detectives.

"Let's go bust some crooks!" Torres said, smiling.

Frank sat in the front seat of Torres's dark blue sedan, staring through the windshield as they made their way uptown. The other two detectives, Johnson and Klaver, were following behind them in another unmarked police car. All along the sidewalks, people were taking advantage of the sunny weather. Street vendors sold cold drinks and hot dogs on almost every corner. Other drivers had their windows rolled down and their stereos cranked up.

"Now, we're only going out there to scout the place out," Torres reminded them. "We're not busting in or anything. We'll sniff around. If I can catch somebody actually duping tapes I'll make an arrest. That way I can make a conviction stick."

Frank nodded. He was glad Peterson had sent them along with Torres, especially since having a warrant would make it legal to search the place. Still, his style would be a little cramped by having to follow someone else's lead.

"So, how do you guys know Chief Peterson, anyway?" Torres asked a little while later.

"He's a friend of our father's, Fenton Hardy. Actually, they used to be partners," Frank explained.

"He's also helped us out on a few other cases," Joe added.

"Cases? What do you mean?" Torres asked, glancing at Joe in the rearview mirror. Suddenly recognition dawned on the detective's face. "Hey, wait a minute. I know you now. You're the

Hardy brothers." Torres let out a low whistle. "What do you know!"

Torres shook his head and grinned, as they left Manhattan through the Midtown Tunnel. When they emerged at the other end, they were in the borough of Queens. After a few short blocks, Torres pulled up and stopped beside the curb.

"We'll go on foot from here," Torres told them, stepping out of the car. "Johnson and Klaver will wait outside the warehouse as backup."

Torres motioned the two plainclothes officers to move into position.

"The warehouse is on the corner," Torres said, pointing up the deserted block. "It's really run-down on the outside. A perfect place for someone who doesn't want to attract attention."

"What's the plan?" Frank asked.

"We walk right in," Torres replied. "Chances are this guy has his front door wide open with his business going on as usual. Besides, I've found that if you just stroll into a place confidently—you know, like you own it—people don't hassle you."

Torres stopped at a dilapidated warehouse. The main door was rusty, and the windows were patched with plywood. A small cardboard sign that read Fanboy Distribution was tacked to the door.

There was a door next to the loading dock.

Frank watched Torres grip the knob and twist it. He smiled as he pulled the door open.

"See?" Torres said. "Commercial premises with unlocked entrances can be crossed by anybody, including the police, at any time."

The trio ventured into the dimly lit warehouse. Frank followed Torres, who stopped short behind a stack of crates and pointed inside. A dozen men were frantically packing boxes. Above these men, in a second-story, glass enclosed office to the side of the large open room, a man with dark hair and a neatly trimmed beard was speaking on the phone.

The man wore a suit, and Frank guessed he was Martinelli. Frank turned his glance back to the main warehouse floor.

The place was crammed with stuff. There were piles of unopened crates, each marked Hong Kong, just like the ones in Chang's warehouse. No wonder Martinelli had to rent space at Chang's. To one side of the room stood a long table loaded with piles and piles of CDs and cassette tapes in clear plastic boxes. In one corner a boy of about twelve was running a copy machine.

Color copies were flying out of the feeder. As another boy picked up the pile of copies, Frank was able to make out two images clearly: a clenched red hand, the Tight Fist logo, and Randy Rand's face.

They were printing covers for counterfeited copies of Randy Rand's tapes and CDs!

Chapter 4

"DO YOU SEE what I see?" Frank whispered to Joe and Torres, pointing to the copier.

Torres nodded. He pulled out a radio from inside his jacket. "Let's go!" he whispered into it. Within seconds Johnson and Klaver entered the warehouse.

"Okay, nobody move!" Torres boomed.

Joe watched as the men stopped and stared at Torres, who was holding his shield high in the air. "Police," Torres shouted, working his way into the crowd. "We're going upstairs," he said. "Johnson, get us some backup," he said as he motioned to the female officer.

"What do you boys make of this?" Torres asked as they approached a table piled high with clear plastic CD cases. The boy who had been making copies was standing with his hands high in the air. The other officer kept guard over the men who had been loading crates.

"As far as I know, most CDs are duped in Hong Kong because of the laser technology that's required," Frank said.

"Right," Joe added. "But tapes are easy to duplicate on any good quality cassette player. Covers for both can be made on color copiers just like the one there."

They hurried up the stairs to the main office. Joe stepped through the door right behind Torres. Frank slipped in next to him. The man with the beard sat behind his desk, his tanned face expressing his amusement.

The office was bare of anything other than a desk and a dirty gray filing cabinet tucked in the corner of the office. The man must have seen the commotion Torres caused, but he was calm and collected.

"Can I help you, officer?" the man said.

"No, but you're going to need some help from a good lawyer," Torres replied. "Are you Jack Martinelli?"

"This is private property, you know," the man said, ignoring the detective's question.

"That's funny," Torres responded. "I didn't see a sign." He turned to Joe and Frank. "Did you guys see a sign? Like one that read Private Property or Do Not Enter?"

Joe and Frank shook their heads.

"No," Torres said. "All I saw was an open warehouse with counterfeit tapes and some guy dressed in a fancy suit who probably knows his rights better than I do. Now, I asked you a question. Are you Jack Martinelli?"

"Yeah, I'm Martinelli, and I know you need a search warrant," Martinelli replied confidently. "It's going to be my counsel's focal point when I sue the city over this."

Torres took a piece of paper from his jacket pocket and put it on Martinelli's desk. "There's your warrant," Torres said with satisfaction.

Joe beamed. "We might just have a record here," he whispered to Frank. "Less than twenty-four hours and this case is as good as solved."

Frank elbowed Joe. "Hold your horses, bro," he shot back in a low tone. "This guy's not going easy."

Martinelli stared at the warrant. "I will only speak with my attorney," he said defiantly.

"That's your right," Torres said politely. "You have the right to remain silent. If you give up that right, anything you say can and will be held against you in a court of law. You have the right to an attorney. If you cannot afford an attorney, one will be appointed to you by a court of law—''

While Torres finished reading him his rights, Martinelli smiled, sitting comfortably in his plush chair. ''Business has its little setbacks,'' he muttered, rising when Torres motioned him to stand.

As Torres started to frisk Martinelli, Joe heard sirens approaching in the distance. ''That's the clean-up crew,'' Torres remarked. ''You guys want a ride back to your hotel?''

''No, that's okay,'' Frank said. ''We'll take a subway back to Tight Fist Records and tell Randy about this.''

''Right,'' said Joe. ''And I think I'll tell Tabitha. She should be pretty happy.''

The Hardys said goodbye to Torres and made their way out of the warehouse. Joe stopped at the table where the boy had been making cassette and CD covers on the color copier.

''These sure look like the real thing,'' Joe said, holding one up. ''This cover is just like the one on my Randy Rand CD.''

Frank grabbed his brother by the jacket. ''Let's get going,'' he said, darting past several officers making their way into the warehouse. ''We're still on a case, remember?''

An hour later Joe and Frank got off a subway a short block from the Tight Fist office. Joe checked the time. It was only one thirty P.M. He wondered if he could talk Frank into staying one more night so he could enjoy the city. Maybe Randy would be so grateful that he'd let them hang around with him some more.

They entered the reception area, said hello to the receptionist, whose name was Bonnie, and headed for the recording studio. The narrow hallway that led to the studio was covered with framed posters of Randy's tours and albums. Frank and Joe opened a door marked Studio One and stepped into the small glass-enclosed control booth where the sound engineer was sitting. Randy and the Power Brokers were in the large section of the studio with their instruments and the live microphones.

The sound engineer was seated behind the sound equipment, and Joe marveled at the array of buttons and switches on the console. "Are they recording?" he asked the woman.

"No," she replied. "They're just rehearsing."

"Shouldn't we go into the studio and tell Randy?" Joe said.

"No," Frank said. "Let's not interrupt him."

Joe nodded. The main sound room that Randy and the Power Brokers were in was totally soundproof.

"It all looks so complicated," Joe said, glancing down at the console in front of the sound engineer.

"It's a pretty elaborate system," the woman agreed. "There are twenty-four tracks on this baby. That means I have twenty-four layers of sound. I can take all the different tracks and combine them on the mixing equipment," she said, demonstrating as she talked. "I can raise the volume of some instruments, lower others, sharpen the tone, and even create sound effects like echoes and fade-outs. Right now I'm working on the last track we laid down."

Joe glanced up then and noticed that the rehearsal had stopped. Randy saw Joe and Frank and spoke into his mike, asking them to come out of the control booth. They excused themselves and left the booth to join Randy and the Power Brokers.

"So what went down, amigos?" Randy asked as the Hardys joined him. He was smiling expectantly.

"Jack Martinelli was busted by the police at a warehouse in Queens," Joe said, explaining what had happened. "Your counterfeiter is currently a guest of the state."

"Righteous!" Randy cheered, giving Joe a high five.

At that moment Tabitha entered the room. "Here you two are," she said to the Hardys. "Bonnie said you headed this way."

Frank told Tabitha what had happened at the warehouse.

"That's fantastic!" Tabitha beamed. "We should celebrate."

"I'm taking these dudes out for a feast," Randy announced. "And, hey—there's a press conference later on to drum up interest in my gig at Madison Square Garden on Friday night. Why don't you hang around for that?"

"Sounds good to me," Joe said, glancing hopefully at Frank.

"Sure, Randy," Frank said with a shrug. "If you can put us up at the hotel one more night, we'll stay in the city tonight and head back to Bayport tomorrow."

"Sounds like a plan if you promise to come back for the show Friday," Randy said. "Now let me take you guys to the finest eatery this side of Brooklyn."

Peter's Gourmet Burger Haven wasn't exactly what Joe would have thought of as a "fine eatery," but he had no qualms about devouring two burgers and a heaping order of fries. Tabitha and Randy sat across from the Hardys, and the four of them talked about Martinelli until it was time to head back to the hotel for Randy's press conference.

When Randy's limousine pulled up to the curb of the Gramercy, a solid wall of fans had to be held back by his security and the police. Photographers snapped away, making Joe see circles of light as he stepped out of the car and was ushered, along with the others, into the hotel.

Once inside, the Hardys were escorted to a large conference room packed with reporters and photographers from television stations, newspapers, and magazines. The crowd of reporters was kept to one side of the room. Immediately they began calling out questions to Randy.

"The press conference will begin in a few minutes," Tabitha called back. "Please reserve your questions until then."

A podium had been set up among stand-up posters of Randy's latest album, *The Powers That B*. Joe was shocked to see a life-size cardboard stand-up of Beastmaster J among the props. He scanned the crowd in the room and spotted the Beastmaster, staring seemingly without blinking at Randy.

"I forgot that Beastmaster J was on the same ticket for the show," Joe muttered to Frank, motioning to the Beastmaster.

"That guy really has it in for Randy," Frank replied.

Joe glanced at Randy, who was in the center of a crowd, shaking hands with what had to be a bunch of corporate bigwigs.

Just then Joe spotted Detective Torres in the crowd. Flashes continued to go off, causing Torres to shield his eyes as he approached the Hardys.

"I thought I'd find you here," Torres said.

"What's up?" Joe asked.

"Martinelli is out on bail," Torres said grimly.

"What?" Frank asked, astonished. "Already?"

Torres nodded. "Already. The guy's got a fancy lawyer. Besides, no judge would hold him without bail on a counterfeiting offense."

"So what happens now?" Joe asked.

"It'll probably be months before his trial," Torres said. "I'm afraid he'll go right back into business. He'll be more careful this time, probably lay low for a few months before finding a new warehouse."

"So he's free to continue ripping Randy off?" Joe said indignantly.

"Not exactly," Torres insisted. "I'm keeping an eye on him. We'll be setting up a new task force to—"

Suddenly Randy Rand appeared behind Torres, his face flushed with anger. "What's this I hear?" he shouted. "That creep Martinelli is out of jail already?"

"Now, Mr. Rand, don't get upset—" Torres began.

"If you can't get this creep to stop ripping me off," Randy shouted, well within earshot of the reporters, "then I will!"

"Randy, wait!" Tabitha cried, pushing her way through the crowd toward him.

"I'm sick of waiting!" Randy screamed. "I

worked hard for this, and I'm not going to let some creep take it all away from me!"

"Be cool, Randy," Joe urged, blocking Randy's exit.

With the mikes on and the photographers clicking away, Randy side armed Joe, knocking him to the ground. Then he kicked over the cardboard stand-up display of the Beastmaster and stormed out of the conference room.

Chapter 5

FRANK STARTED to follow Randy.

"No," Tabitha said, reaching for Frank's arm to stop him. "Let him go. He needs to blow off some steam."

Frank glanced back over his shoulder and noticed that Beastmaster J was staring at them from across the room with a huge smirk on his face.

The reporters were buzzing around Beastmaster, asking him about Randy's outburst.

"Hey, doesn't anybody care about me?" Joe asked, standing up and brushing himself off.

"Sorry," Torres said apologetically. "I had no idea the guy would take it so hard."

"Is there anything else we can do?" Joe asked.

Torres let out a loud sigh. "The best we can do is keep tabs on Martinelli. His material was confiscated, so he'll have to import more CDs into the country. Until he tries something and we catch him at it, he's a free man."

"If you catch him with more goods, will that shut him down?" Frank asked.

"It might only slow him down a bit. I know of cases where people go to jail and continue to run their illegal activities from behind bars."

"This all seems so unfair," Tabitha said, setting her mouth in a straight line.

"I agree," Torres said. "But trust me—Martinelli isn't as slick as he thinks he is. I'll get him eventually."

"I'll talk to my lawyer again," Tabitha said. "Maybe there's something else we can do."

"That's a good idea," Torres replied. "Listen, Frank, Joe—I'll keep you and Ms. Cowan posted. If you can't get me that autograph," Torres added with a shrug, "I understand, considering what's happened."

Tabitha grinned for the first time in several minutes. "I'll get Randy to autograph his new CD for you. After all you've done, it's the least we can do."

"Thanks," Torres said, smiling brightly. "I sure would appreciate that." He checked his watch. "I've got to head home. It's been a long day."

After Torres left, Tabitha asked Frank and Joe, "What are you guys up to tonight?"

"Nothing," Frank said with a shrug.

"I have some business to wrap up at the office," Tabitha said. "Why don't you meet me there later, and I'll give you the grand tour."

"That would be great," Joe replied, grinning from ear to ear.

"In about an hour?" Tabitha asked.

With Torres and his men gone, the private security guards were no longer able to hold the reporters back.

"Oh, no, it's the news hounds," Tabitha said, noticing them straining to approach her. "What should I tell them?"

Before Frank could answer, the reporters started hurling questions at her.

"Why did Randy storm out of here?"

"Ms. Cowan, is it true that you and Randy are romantically involved?"

"Ms. Cowan, how many strings is your affluent father pulling for you?"

"How serious is the feud between Randy and Beastmaster J?"

"If I were you," Frank whispered, "I'd head for the exit."

Tabitha turned to Frank and Joe. "Help me out of here, guys, and fast."

* * *

It was after seven o'clock when Frank and Joe hopped off a bus just a couple of blocks from Tight Fist Records. They had killed time by eating at a small Chinese restaurant near their hotel.

"I like Tabitha," Joe confessed as he and Frank walked toward the studio. "She's different, and I really admire her for running her own business."

"She sure seems to know what she's doing," Frank agreed, as he glanced around, checking out the neighborhood. "Is it my imagination," Frank said, "or is everyone down here wearing black?"

Joe completely ignored Frank, asking, "Do you think I should ask Tabitha out?"

"I don't know, Joe. She's beautiful, rich—she's a little out of your league, don't you think?" Frank teased.

"That's never stopped me before," Joe said with a grin.

Frank and Joe headed up the steps of Tight Fist Records and entered the quiet building. The receptionist was gone for the evening. The Hardys made their way to Tabitha's office, where they found her busy at her desk.

"How's it going?" Joe asked, knocking lightly on her open door.

Tabitha raised her head from her work and smiled. "Hi, guys."

She set her work to one side and rose from her chair. She was wearing jeans, a black T-shirt, and a vest covered with buttons that had the Tight Fist logo on them—a clenched red fist.

"I hope we're not interrupting," Frank said.

"Oh, no," Tabitha said, stretching. "I hate working with numbers. I could shoot my bookkeeper for taking her vacation this week."

"If you're busy," Joe said, "we can—"

"Don't be silly," Tabitha said. "I need a break, and I'd like to give you guys a tour."

"Have you heard anything from Randy?" Joe asked.

"No," Tabitha said with a frown. "He's probably hanging out somewhere, fuming. He'll call after he cools off. He has a really hot temper, you know. You should see the tantrums he throws in the studio if things aren't just right."

"He seems so mellow, though," Frank said.

"He is for the most part, but he's got a temper, too," Tabitha said.

The Hardys and Tabitha stepped out of her office just as two young men came strolling down the narrow hallway. They were whispering to each other but stopped abruptly when they saw Tabitha with Frank and Joe. Frank studied them. One was short with long, dark hair that hung down his back. The other had long hair, too, but his was blond, and he looked like a bodybuilder. Both men were dressed in dark jeans and Tight Fist T-shirts with Tight Fist buttons pinned to them.

The men stopped in front of Tabitha. "We're heading out now, Tabitha," the blond muscular man said, smiling at Frank and Joe.

"Okay, Keith," Tabitha replied. "Oh, by the way, this is Frank and Joe Hardy. They were the ones who helped catch that Martinelli creep. Guys, this is Keith Steiner and Mike Rigani. They're sound engineers."

"Pleasure," Mike said.

Keith tossed back his blond hair and gave the Hardys a brief wave. "Catch you later, dudes," he said.

Keith and Mike continued out of the building. At the same time the phone in Tabitha's office started ringing.

"Hold on a second, guys," Tabitha said, stepping back into her office.

Tabitha hadn't been gone two seconds before the Hardys heard her shouting from inside her office.

"But, Daddy, that's not fair!" Tabitha cried. "You're so mean! I'm not a little girl anymore. I said I would keep this business alive, and I meant it. Just you wait and see!"

"It sounds like your princess has a split personality," Frank whispered to Joe after Tabitha's voice became inaudible again.

After another minute or so, Tabitha stepped

back into the hallway. Her mouth was set and she looked as if she'd been crying.

"I really hate to disappoint you," she said glumly, "but your tour of the studio will have to wait. My father saw bits of the press conference on the news and I've got to spend a couple of hours assuring him the family name won't be tarnished by this whole affair."

"We understand," Frank said, glancing at Joe. Frank knew his brother had to be disappointed.

"Yeah," Joe added. "Besides, we have to get an early start tomorrow."

"Thanks for understanding," Tabitha said. "And believe me, I'd much rather spend my evening giving you a tour. My father can be a real bore."

Frank and Joe let Tabitha go back in her office and headed out of the studio.

"Sorry, Joe," Frank said once they were back on the street. "At least this visit wasn't a total loss. I'd say that was a pretty interesting tantrum we just overheard. I wonder what it means?" Frank mused.

"What are you talking about?" Joe asked. "This case is closed, remember?"

Within fifteen minutes the Hardys were back at their hotel checking on Randy Rand. Frank rapped lightly on his door. There was no answer.

"What should we do?" Frank asked. "I can't

help feeling responsible for Randy. Maybe we should try to find him."

"I can understand why Randy's so upset," Joe said. "There seems to be a real lack of justice in this case."

"Torres said he'd get Martinelli eventually," Frank reminded Joe. "If Martinelli goes back into business, he'll wind up being tried on two counts of counterfeiting. He'll get time and, if he's smart, find an honest trade."

"In the meantime, though, he'll still be making money off Randy," Joe argued. "And what if he drives Tight Fist out of business before he goes to trial? What's fair about that?"

"So, do you have any bright ideas?" Frank asked.

"Not really," Joe said. "But until I get one, I say we go back to Martinelli's warehouse."

Frank looked at Joe with surprise. "Why?"

"Randy was pretty ticked off when he left the press conference. Remember when he said he was tired of waiting? Maybe he's planning to confront Martinelli himself."

"You may be right," Frank said. "We have one more night here—we might as well put it to good use."

Less than an hour later Frank and Joe were walking the deserted block between the subway and Jack Martinelli's warehouse. Joe kept glancing behind them and picking up his pace. Finally Frank grabbed Joe's arm and said, "What's the matter with you?"

"I can't shake the feeling that we're being watched or followed," Joe said, pivoting around to take in the dark sidewalk behind them.

"The street is empty," Frank said. "If we were being followed, we'd have noticed by now."

"I'm not so sure," Joe insisted, stopping at the entrance to the warehouse. "Frank, something tells me we're being tailed."

Frank stared back down the dark expanse of street. "Do you want to go back now?" he asked.

Joe didn't answer. Instead, he pointed to a side door of the warehouse. It was wide open.

"I don't have a good feeling about this," Joe said, shaking his head slowly. "It's almost like someone is waiting for us."

"Don't forget about Randy," Frank said. "If he's here, he could be in big trouble."

"You're right," Joe said, taking a deep breath. "Let's do it."

Frank and Joe entered the dark warehouse. Above them a single light burned in Martinelli's office. They silently took the stairs, ready to spring into action at the first sign of trouble.

When they reached the door, they saw it was open a crack. Frank turned to Joe. There could be someone waiting for them inside. Should they take the chance?

Joe nodded yes. Frank broke into a light sweat. Who knew what they'd find inside? He silently counted to three on his fingers. On three, he and Joe burst into the office.

Frank pulled up short. He stood motionless, focusing on the back of a still form sprawled across the floor a few feet in front of him. Frank recognized the dark hair and beard in profile. With a start, he realized he was staring at a corpse—the corpse of Jack Martinelli.

Chapter 6

JOE LOOKED closely at Martinelli's body. The man had fallen face first to the floor, and the right side of his ashen face was pressed against the cold linoleum. There was a nasty gunshot wound at the base of his skull.

"Look," Joe said, pointing to the wound.

"I know," Frank said somberly, his hands at his waist, surveying the situation. "Don't touch anything," he warned Joe.

Joe took a deep breath to calm his queasy stomach. Now wasn't the time to be sick. There were valuable clues here, and he had to stay alert in order to find them.

"It looks as though he was hit with something with a small caliber," Joe said, studying the wound. "It didn't leave much of an exit wound. Couldn't be over a thirty-eight."

"Let's see if we can find another phone and call Torres," Frank said.

"Good idea," Joe agreed. On the way downstairs, he stayed on guard just in case the person who killed Martinelli was still hanging around. Frank found a phone next to the copy machine, picked it up, and dialed Torres's number at the precinct.

"They're going to call him at home and send over some cops from the local precinct," Frank said after he hung up. "They should be here any minute."

Joe nodded grimly. "In that case we should look around until they get here."

"That makes sense," Frank said, and headed up the stairs again.

Back in Martinelli's office, Joe searched the room with his eyes, careful not to touch or disturb anything. Frank did the same.

"Nothing seems to be out of place," Joe remarked.

Frank nodded. "No sign of a disturbance either," he said. "Martinelli was obviously taken by surprise."

Joe was about to suggest they search another part of the warehouse when something caught his eye. "Hey, Frank," he said, "check this out."

Joe led Frank to the corner closest to the doorway. A round white object about an inch across, lay on the floor. Joe knelt down to take a closer look. It was a metal button, the kind that had a pin across the back, and it had a clenched red fist on it—the Tight Fist Records logo!

"Everyone at Tight Fist wears these buttons," Frank said excitedly. "Tabitha, Randy—even the sound engineers."

"I'd guess whoever committed the murder dropped this," Joe said. A horrible thought crept through his brain. "Frank, we came here to find Randy. Instead we find a corpse and a Tight Fist Records button. You know how this looks?"

Frank let out a low whistle. "I'd say Randy is a suspect. He practically threatened Martinelli at that press conference."

"Let's just hope he's got an alibi," Joe said. "I know they say Randy is a hothead, but I can't believe he'd commit murder."

"I like Randy, too," Frank admitted. "But considering how mad he was earlier tonight, there's no telling what he might have done."

Joe heard sirens moving closer. He and Frank went back down to the first floor and saw Torres enter through the open side door. Several uniformed men spilled in behind the detective, along with two men in plain clothes. One wore glasses and carried a leather satchel. The other was a massive man who peered around the warehouse with a keen, trained gaze.

"Frank, Joe," Torres said, motioning to the man with glasses. "This is Fred Archer, the medical examiner, and this other gentleman is Simon Grant, a homicide detective from the Queens district. They'll both be asking you a few questions."

"Where's the body?" Archer asked.

"In the office upstairs," Joe said.

"How long have you been here?" Grant asked gruffly. "And more important, why are you here?"

"We came here to help a client of ours, Randy Rand," Frank said. "We've been here about twenty minutes."

"You wanted to help Randy do what exactly?" Grant asked dubiously.

"Lay off, Simon," Torres said sternly. "These kids are friends of Chief Peterson. They're not up to anything."

"We'll see about that," Grant remarked. "Do you kids know where your friend Rand is by any chance?"

"No," Joe replied. He was about to mention that they had come to the warehouse looking for Randy, but thought better of it.

"Don't go anywhere," Grant said, and followed Archer upstairs.

"You're lucky I live right here in Queens, or you two would have to deal with Grant by yourselves," Torres said. "He's a good cop with a tough personality. He likes to investigate every angle, and sometimes he works from the premise that people are guilty until proven innocent."

"Nice guy," Frank said, making a face.

"I'm sure he doesn't want any help from us 'kids,' but there's something we should tell you," Joe said. "We found something upstairs." He told Torres about the button.

Torres shook his head sadly, took out his notepad, and wrote down the information. "Exhibit A," he replied. "Things aren't looking too good for Rand. As soon as you called me, I had to put out an all-points bulletin for him."

Joe saw Archer and Grant coming down the stairs. Archer ambled over to them and said, "My official opinion will have to wait for a complete autopsy, but unofficially the gunshot wound appears to be the cause of death. I'd say time of death was between seven and eight o'clock." Archer rubbed his eyes. "I'm no cop, but I'd say it's a mob hit."

"Randy Rand still has to be a suspect because of the public threats he made," Grant said, appearing by his side and adding his opinion.

"Okay," Torres called out. "I want every square inch of this warehouse searched. We've got men posted at Rand's hotel, and I want a massive search for him. Talk to anyone who might know him, give us an address of a known hangout."

"We better head back to the hotel ourselves,"

Frank whispered to his brother. "I want to hear Randy's story. Let's just hope he hasn't left town."

Joe nodded and began to follow Frank out of the warehouse.

"Not so fast," Grant called after them. "Tell me where you live. I'll come by tonight to question you."

Joe gave Grant the name of their hotel and their room number before he and Frank stepped outside. Joe squinted at the convoy of police cars lined up with their flashers revolving.

"Not good," Joe murmured softly, thinking of Randy Rand. "Not good at all."

Joe and Frank were lucky to find a cab to take them back to their hotel. While they rode the hotel elevator to the fourth floor, Joe thought long and hard about the case. He was upset that his current favorite musician was a murder suspect.

"Some trip this turned out to be," Joe said as the elevator doors opened. "I thought we had ourselves an open-and-shut case and would spend our last night hanging out with Randy Rand and Tabitha. Now we're caught in the middle of a murder investigation."

Joe and Frank saw the two plainclothes police officers standing vigil at Randy's door immediately. One was a short man with red hair, the other a tall, black-haired woman. Frank and Joe walked toward Randy's room.

"Is Randy back yet?" Frank asked.

"Not yet," the male officer replied. Joe saw the name Field on his badge. "Are you guys Frank and Joe Hardy?" the man asked.

"Yes," Joe replied cautiously.

"We were told by Detective Grant to ask the two of you a few questions."

"Such as?" Frank replied.

"Do you have any idea where Randy Rand is?" the woman officer, whose name was Chun asked.

"No," Joe replied, exasperated. "Grant already asked us that. If we did, we would have told him where to find Randy. We found Martinelli's body. If we were involved, why would we report the murder and stay at the scene?"

"Nobody's accusing you of anything," Officer Chun replied. "We're only trying to get to the bottom of this."

Just then Joe heard the elevator doors open. A disheveled Randy Rand stepped out and made his way to room 420.

"Excuse us," Chun said. She and Field quickly intercepted Randy.

"Mr. Rand?" Field said. He and Chun produced their IDs and held them up in front of Randy's bloodshot eyes. "Let's go into your room. We have a few questions to ask you."

"About what?" Randy said, staring helplessly at the Hardys. "Am I under arrest?"

"We only want to ask you a few questions at this point, Mr. Rand," Chun said, steering Randy by the arm toward his room.

"Why?" Randy asked, his voice thick with confusion.

"You're a suspect in the murder of Jack Martinelli."

"Martinelli is dead?" Randy said. "You're kidding me. I didn't kill anyone. I was out walking. I always do that when I need to clear my head."

"Were you with anyone? Did you go anywhere where people may have seen you?" Chun asked.

"No," Randy muttered solemnly, eyes focused on the carpet. "I was just walking."

"Come with us, please," Field said, leading Randy into his room. "That will be all, gentlemen," he said sternly, shutting the door on the Hardys.

Joe and Frank slowly walked back to their room. "I wish we could be in there with him," Joe said. "I won't sleep until I know what Randy's story is."

"It didn't seem like Randy had much of a story," Frank said. "Or much of a chance convincing the police he's innocent. What do you think, Joe?"

"I don't know," Joe replied, opening the room door and turning on the light. "I want to believe that Randy's innocent, but only a blind man or fool would deny that he's a suspect."

The Hardys weren't in their room too long before they heard a loud pounding on their door.

"What now?" Joe muttered, opening the door.

Detective Grant stood in the doorway, his face red with anger. "I know you boys are friends of Peterson," the man said roughly, "but if I find out you're trying to cover up for Rand in any way, shape, or form, the two of you are going to be in as much trouble as he is!"

Chapter 7

FRANK COULDN'T believe what he was hearing.

"We hardly know Randy Rand," Frank protested. "Even if he were our closest friend, we wouldn't cover for him."

Frank glanced at Joe, who looked ready to explode. "We're on your side." Joe said, his face bright red now. "Why are you accusing us of being accessories to murder?"

Grant leaned in and stuck a finger in Joe's face. "I've got a dead body on the way to the morgue and a suspect who says he has insomnia. I'm going to squeeze whoever I need to get some answers around here. I'm just warning you—if you're involved, you're going down. If you have something to say to me, you'd better say it now."

"I do have something to say," Joe muttered. "Good night." He closed the door in Grant's face.

"Okay," Grant shouted through the door. "But remember—you've had your opportunity. I'm going back to talk to that young punk friend of yours."

Frank let out a long sigh. "We'd better question Randy when Grant's finished with him," he suggested. "That is, if they don't take him into custody."

Frank and Joe paced their room for what seemed like hours. Finally they heard the low murmurs of Grant, Field, and Chun in the hall as they were leaving Randy's room.

"Let's go," Frank said after he heard the elevator doors slide shut. He stepped out of the room with Joe right behind him. The hallway was quiet. Frank rapped lightly on Randy's door.

"Randy?" Frank called out. "It's Frank and Joe."

Randy opened the door, and Frank and Joe stepped inside. Before Frank could open his mouth, Randy said, "I'm scared, man." A look of stark terror on his face, Randy danced around nervously. "They're going to pin this on me, and I didn't do it. I swear I'm innocent. You've got to help me. Stay on a few extra days. Prove to them I'm innocent."

"Okay, Randy," Frank said, gently putting his hands on Randy's shoulders. "But first, you've got to calm down and help us. Can you think of anyone who may be able to prove you weren't at the murder scene?"

"I just can't think straight right now," Randy said, pacing the room. "My mind is racing."

"That's okay, man," Joe said. "Just try to get it together."

"Did you talk to anybody?" Frank prodded. "Grab a bite someplace where they might remember you?"

Randy kept marching back and forth. "No, no. I just walked around. I didn't talk to anybody."

"Maybe we should do this tomorrow," Joe said.

"I think you're right," Frank said.

Randy closed his eyes and pressed his hands to his face. "Maybe I'll remember more tomorrow," he said. "Catch me at Tight Fist. I should be there after ten or so." He walked Frank and Joe to the door and opened it for them. "Thanks, guys," Randy said wearily. "Thanks a lot."

The Hardys headed back to their room. "Do you think he's telling the truth?" Frank asked when they got inside.

Joe shook his head thoughtfully. "I hope so, for his sake. I guess it's for us to find out."

"As always," Frank said with a sigh.

The next morning Randy had room service send breakfast to Frank and Joe. As they demolished french toast and bacon, they did some brainstorming about the case.

"I can't get that button out of my mind," Joe said, mopping the last of his syrup dry with a piece of french toast. "Finding it was too easy. What if it was planted?"

"Maybe someone was trying to frame Randy?" Frank offered.

"Yeah," Joe said, brightening at the thought. "Maybe someone like the Beastmaster. He was at the press conference and knew how easy it would be to frame Randy."

"That sounds kind of farfetched," Frank said, finishing off his orange juice. "Still, the Beastmaster really does have it in for Randy. Of course, Randy could have dropped the pin himself," Frank reminded his brother. "Tabitha was wearing a lot of those pins, too," he continued.

"If the murder took place between seven and eight, Tabitha was with us during that time," Joe reminded Frank. "Besides, why would Tabitha frame Randy? He's her meal ticket. Tight Fist would crumble without him on its label."

"Remember what Archer said? That Martinelli's shooting could have been mob related?" Frank added. "What if Blue Lou Chang had something to do with it? If Chang is a rival counterfeiter, maybe he didn't appreciate Martinelli doing business in town, too."

"Makes sense," Joe agreed. "Let's go to Tight Fist and question Randy and Tabitha."

The Hardys dressed and headed out of the hotel, walking south in the direction of Tight Fist. The day was sunny and clear. They were in the East Village, just a few blocks from Tight Fist, when Frank again noticed Joe glancing around with a disturbed expression on his face.

"What's up?" Frank asked.

"I think we're being followed," Joe said.

"Not again!" Frank joked.

Joe made a face. "Seriously, Frank. When I turned around, I caught a glimpse of someone ducking into a doorway."

Frank turned and followed his brother's gaze, but saw only small knots of people hurrying down the sidewalk. "How could you make out any special movement in that crowd?" Frank said.

"I could have sworn we were being followed," Joe insisted. "Maybe it was just a reflection or something."

"It's easy to get edgy in a situation like this," Frank replied. They had arrived at Tight Fist, and Frank led the way into the building. "Let's talk to Randy first. Oh, Joe, do me a favor."

"What's that?"

"Don't mention the button we found, just in case Randy really is guilty."

"Okay by me."

Bonnie, the receptionist, informed them that Randy and Tabitha were expecting them. The Hardys went to Tabitha's office, where Randy was pensively lying back in a plush recliner. Tabitha was sitting upright behind her desk, her mouth turned down in a grim expression. There were promotional posters on the walls, including one for *The Powers That B*. Above Tabitha's desk was a framed portrait of herself. Frank noticed that most of Tabitha's desk accessories had her name on them—her pens, pencils, and even her coffee mug. This was one woman who seemed pretty fond of herself, Frank mused.

"Come on in," Tabitha said, her voice thin and strained. The record company owner looked tired, as if her troubles had kept her up all night. Frank noted that Randy didn't look much better. He wore the same clothes he'd had on the night before.

"Do you have any good news for me?" Randy asked expectantly.

"We have a notion or two," Frank replied.

"We think you could have been framed by someone," Joe elaborated. "We definitely suspect Beastmaster J."

"Beastmaster J?" Tabitha said, shocked.

"There's major bad blood between you," Frank said to Randy. "He saw your outburst at the press conference. What better way to have the upcoming show at the Garden to himself?"

"Look, Frank," Randy interjected. "I think the Beastmaster is a jerk, but I don't think he'd whack anyone like that."

"You never know," Frank said, puzzled by Randy's sudden defense of his rival. If Randy were guilty, wouldn't he try to encourage suspicion of the Beastmaster instead of sticking up for him?

"We also think that Blue Lou Chang might be involved," Joe added. "Martinelli cornered the dupe market on your CDs and tapes. Maybe Chang decided to take over his business. He probably saw your press conference. With you raving the way you were, Randy, you could have given him or someone else the green light to kill Martinelli, knowing you'd be the main suspect."

"I know," Randy said, embarrassed. "Me and my big mouth."

"That's all we have to go on at this point," Frank said. "We thought we might go check out Chang's warehouse again. See if we can find any evidence against him."

"Sounds good," Tabitha said approvingly. "Because we all know Randy is innocent."

"Thanks, Tabby," Randy said with a weak smile.

Frank and Joe said their goodbyes, agreeing to check in later, and left the studio.

"Are you ready to head to Chinatown?" Frank asked.

"Only if we can grab lunch there," Joe reminded his brother.

"But we had Chinese food last night," Frank reminded him.

"Good point. How about some brick-oven pizza? We can't get that in Bayport," Joe said.

"Sounds great!" Frank said.

Forty-five minutes later Frank and Joe were sitting in the Original Sal's Brick Oven Pizzeria with a pepperoni pie and a couple of sodas in front of them.

"This was a great idea, Joe," Frank said, when the last slice had been put away. "Now we'd better get down to business. There's a subway station about three blocks away."

Once underground, Frank bought the tokens, then led Joe to the right track.

"Are you worried about going back to Chang's warehouse?" Joe asked his brother. "I mean, Torres said Blue Lou plays hardball."

"We'll just play the mob go-between angle again. Claim we represent a potential investor. I don't think Chang will suspect us of being anything else. Besides, his entire gang consists of teenagers. Remember what Torres said? He's used to young guys as gofers."

Frank stood close to the edge of the platform, staring down the tunnel in the direction the train would come from. Joe made his way toward a magazine stand a few feet away.

"There's a new issue of *Rapbeat* with Randy on the cover," Joe called out to Frank. "I'm going to check it out while we're waiting."

Frank leaned against a metal support post and waited at the platform edge for Joe to pay for the magazine. There were a few people standing near him, staring blankly at the tracks, willing the train to come. One man in a raincoat and large floppy hat was pushing a small grocery cart along the platform. Frank wondered if he was homeless.

A cold breeze ran through the tunnel, and Frank heard the train coming. He glanced around for Joe, who was still fishing in his pockets for change to buy the magazine.

"Come on, Joe," Frank called out, watching as the front of the train grew larger.

The train was getting close, and the tracks started to vibrate.

"Come on, Joe!" Frank exclaimed, turning around.

The man in the raincoat was right beside Frank now. Frank was just starting to ask him if he needed help, when the man suddenly shoved his cart aside.

Before Frank could do anything, the man pressed his hands against Frank's chest and pushed him down toward the track bed—right into the path of the oncoming train!

Chapter 8

FRANK DIDN'T FALL, though. He managed to wrap his arms around the post he was standing next to before plunging off the platform. He pulled himself safely back onto the platform as the train pulled up, brushing against him. The man in the raincoat tore into a run and sped off toward the far end of the platform, pushing people out of the way on either side of him.

"Frank!" Joe shouted, racing to his brother.

Joe found his brother squatting on the concrete, his back against the post. As the doors of the train opened, people getting on and off stepped around the brothers. Frank managed to stand up, still propped against the post. He was covered in sweat and shaking profusely.

Joe grabbed him by the shoulders. "Frank, are you okay?" he asked.

"He's getting away, Joe," Frank said, finding his voice and pointing toward his assailant. "We've got to stop him."

With that, new energy flowed through Frank and he took off at a clip. Joe had no idea how his brother did it. Maybe just the thought of the guy who had tried to kill him had pumped Frank's blood with adrenaline. Frank tore after the assailant, Joe fast on his tail.

Joe brushed by the small crowd forming on the platform as he tried to keep the suspect in sight. The assailant outmaneuvered them and at the last possible second bolted for the subway car and jumped in with the doors closing behind him. With a grinding metal screech, the train pulled out of the station.

Joe ran up to where Frank was standing. The two Hardys watched the red lights of the train disappear as it slid deeper into the darkness.

"Did you get a look at him?" Frank asked, panting.

Joe shook his head. "It could have been anybody underneath that floppy hat. Are you sure you're okay?"

"Yeah," Frank said reassuringly. "Just had a couple of years of life scared out of me. If I ever find out who that guy was, I'll put him in traction."

A young couple came over. "Are you okay?" the woman asked. "We saw what happened."

"I'm fine," Frank said. "Thanks."

"We could call the police," the man volunteered.

"Don't worry about it," Frank said, smiling.

Joe assured them that his brother was all right and they walked away.

"If I hadn't grabbed that post, they'd be scraping me off the tracks right now," Frank said.

"I told you I thought we were being followed," Joe said. "Believe me now?"

"I'm not sure," Frank shrugged. "People have been pushed onto the tracks by crazy people before. Maybe that's what happened."

"It's also possible it has something to do with our case," Joe added. "Maybe someone doesn't want it solved."

"Do you think Randy could be behind it?" Frank asked.

"I don't think so. Why wouldn't he just take us off the case? Maybe it was the Beastmaster," Joe suggested almost to himself. "Or Blue Lou Chang. Who's behind this, Frank? Who are we starting to make edgy?"

"As soon as the next train comes, we'll try to find out," Frank said.

Frank and Joe walked the familiar route through the West Side warehouse district to

h my brother onto the subway track
Joe asked gruffly.
ng had something up his sleeve, Joe fi
re was no reason to avoid a confrontatior
t are you talking about?" Chang aske
ly. "I said I had you followed. Ther
no orders to harm you. What are yo
ating?"
e wasn't insinuating anything," Frank saic
g at Joe. "He was asking straight ou
ve been experiencing some strange thing
New York can be a strange town."
I don't like accusations," Chang said, his ex
ssion hardening even more. He stared d
tly into Joe's eyes. "You better be carefu
hat you say," he said simply but emphatically
Joe decided to ask Chang about his associa
ion with Jack Martinelli. "Did you know a ma
named Martinelli?" he said.

"I've heard of him. Why?" Chang replied.

"He was killed last night," Joe said. "Car you think of anyone who might have wanted him dead?"

"Every businessman makes enemies," Chang said. "It comes with the territory. Who knows?"

Frank tried to warn Joe to cool it, but he was too late. Joe was already asking Chang another question. "Was he an enemy of yours, Mr. Chang?" Joe said, going for the score.

Chang abruptly turned away from the Hardys

Chang's warehouse. It was midafternoon by now, and the day was really heating up. The humid air had the boys' shirts sticking to their backs. The street was crowded with warehouse workers pushing dollies loaded with goods in and out of trucks.

They turned the final corner and Joe saw they were at Chang's warehouse. "Are we sticking to the same story?" he asked.

"Yes," Frank replied. "We're errand boys for a Miami mobster."

"Got it," Joe said.

Joe followed Frank to the loading dock door of the warehouse. Two young men wearing black baseball caps with blue snakes emblazoned on them were standing guard at the door. Joe recognized one of them as Andy, the guy who had tried to hit him with the crate during their first visit to the warehouse.

"Hey, Andy," Joe said, hoping the guy wouldn't try to get even for the wrestling hold he had put on him. "What's up?"

"Mr. Chang is expecting you," Andy said coldly. He and the other kid stepped aside to make way for Frank and Joe. "Upstairs. His office is on your right. Third door."

"Thanks," Frank said, casting a surprised glance at Joe.

They stepped into the warehouse. Joe was surprised to see that it was abandoned. All the merchandise they had seen before was gone. Joe wondered if Chang had moved it when Andy told him about Frank and himself. Or maybe the shipment had just been delivered according to schedule. Either way, no evidence.

"Stay on your guard," Frank warned. "We have no idea what we're getting into."

Joe followed Frank up the stairs to Chang's office. The door was closed, so Joe knocked lightly on it.

"Come in," Chang beckoned from inside.

Joe and Frank stepped inside. Chang stood across the room, his back to the Hardys. The man was staring at a framed oil painting on the wall of his plush office. Along with the expensive-looking painting, Chang had an antique Persian rug on the dark-tiled floor. A huge black desk that appeared to be made of ebony stood against the left wall. The desk was clear except for a single phone and one manila folder. On the right wall was a plush couch and a couple of hand-carved arm chairs.

Chang turned to face the Hardys. Joe was surprised to see that Blue Lou was young. He wore wire-rimmed glasses, had dark hair and eyes, and was short but strongly built. There was also an obvious air of power about him.

"Mr. Chang," Frank began. "We represent a man from—"

"You can save your breath," Chang inter-

rupted, sizing the Ha
what sort of mood the
relaxed. Confident. Cur
tacked on your last visit—
to me on television the oth
are conducting some inv
Rand?"

Joe hoped the surprise he
on his face. There was no w
Blue Lou now. "Yes, we are,
estly. "And your man attacked

"You were trespassing," Chan
"Andy was within his rights. He
He protects the company."

"Mr. Chang," Frank interjected.
outside that you were expecting us."

"Yes, Frank and Joe Hardy. I was
replied, offering the Hardys a seat on
Joe sat next to Frank as Chang conti
stand. "I don't take visits from uninvited
lightly," Chang explained. "I don't like p
sniffing around. I built this organization with
own blood and sweat, and when someone show
up unasked I find out everything I can about
him. Members of my youth club followed you."

Joe turned to Frank, who nodded slightly. So he was right! They had been followed. Even though Joe was trying to keep a level head, he suddenly thought of Frank's narrow escape on the subway. "One of your men didn't happen to

try to pu
did he?"
If Cha
ured the
"Wh
curious
were
insinu
"H
starin
We'
But

to contemplate the painting on the wall. He spoke with his back to Joe and Frank.

"My business, and my enemies, are of no concern to you. You've worn out your welcome along with my patience. Please leave."

Joe opened his mouth to speak, but Frank tugged on his arm. "Not now," Frank muttered. "Let's just get out of here."

Joe followed Frank out of the office and back out onto the street. "What do you think?" Joe asked after they were out of earshot of the guards.

"A major possibility," Frank replied. "He seems like the kind of guy who'd enjoy taking revenge on his enemies. Which now probably includes us, thanks to you and your big mouth."

"He already knew about us," Joe protested. "Why try to lie again? He must have known we suspected him of Martinelli's murder."

"I'm not so sure," Frank said. "He seemed really offended by your accusation. I don't think he was acting."

"I think he was just ticked off because he knows we're onto him," Joe insisted. "Trying to scare us with borderline threats. He won't do anything. He's just blowing smoke."

"What if he did instruct someone to take us down?" Frank wondered. "What if that subway incident was his idea? Joe, this guy might be seriously gunning for us."

Joe turned the possibility around in his head. If Blue Lou was out to get them, or even just scare them, Joe had just antagonized him further. Something in all this didn't make sense, though. "If Chang really wanted us out of the picture, we'd probably be dead by now," Joe pointed out.

Frank let out a deep breath. "That's a nice way of looking at things, Joe," he said gruffly.

"Sorry," said Joe. "Look, why don't we take a cab? I'd say we've had more than enough of subways for one day, huh?"

Frank laughed and held his arm out to hail the next cab that drove by. During the ride back to the hotel, Joe sat silently, remembering that Torres had described Chang as a hardball player. Don't sweat it, he thought to himself. Chang won't come after us. No way.

Joe and Frank took the elevator to the fourth floor. Joe had managed to put his fears concerning Blue Lou aside and was ready for a short nap before dinner.

"I know we're tired," Frank said, "but let's work out a game plan."

"Okay," Joe said sleepily, and walked over to the beds, pulling off his shirt. He glanced down at Frank's bed, and his eyes widened.

Stuck in Frank's pillow was a knife with a black handle. The handle was hand carved with a snake that was painted blue. It was exactly like the ones on the caps worn by Blue Lou Chang's youth gang!

Chapter 9

"UH, FRANK," Joe Hardy said. "Aren't hotels supposed to leave mints on the pillows?"

"What are you talking about?" Frank asked, walking up behind Joe and peering over his shoulder. Then he saw the knife that was pinning his pillow in place.

"A calling card," Frank said grimly. He reached in his pocket for a handkerchief and gently pulled the knife out of the pillow. "And a warning," Frank added, examining the knife carefully. "Seems we got Chang's attention."

"The guy's sort of melodramatic," Joe said. While frightened just a few seconds earlier, Joe now was getting angry. "I don't like being played with like this, Frank," he muttered.

"Me either," Frank agreed. "But we have to expect this sort of threat from a criminal like Blue Lou."

"If it was Blue Lou," Joe added, "then we're on the right track."

"We don't have an explanation for the Tight Fist pin, though," Frank said.

"Let's clue Randy in on this," Joe suggested. "I hope he's back from the studio."

Frank and Joe knocked on Randy's door. The rap star opened it for them and quickly ushered them inside.

"Have you guys got anything?" Randy asked expectantly. Under his eyes were dark shadows, from not sleeping, Frank supposed. Being under suspicion for something so serious was taking a toll on him.

"We have a solid suspect," Joe announced hopefully. "Blue Lou Chang. He gave us the runaround and then demanded that we leave."

"He admitted that he had some of his gang follow us," Frank continued. "Some lunatic tried to push me in front of a subway earlier. I think now it was probably one of Chang's boys. After we questioned Blue Lou about Martinelli, we came back here to find this buried in my pillow."

Frank showed the knife to Randy. "Be careful, dudes," Randy said, his eyes suddenly bright. "This guy sounds dangerous. Maybe I should get some security for you."

"We're not worried," Joe said. "It was just a warning. Besides, if Chang wants to try something, we have to let him and catch him in the act. We just have to be careful."

"So what now?" Randy asked.

"Next on our list is the Beastmaster," Frank replied. "We want to question him. As soon as possible."

"I know where he rehearses," Randy offered. "But I also know that you won't be able to get in to see him until tomorrow."

Frank must have looked disappointed because Randy punched him lightly on the shoulder. "Man, don't be so down. I'll hook you up with the locale, promise. Meanwhile, why don't we three check out some action tonight. There are a couple of acts I've been meaning to catch."

"All right!" Joe cheered. "We can hang out."

Frank didn't want to let Joe down. "Maybe a break is what we all need right now."

"You bet it is," Randy said.

Frank and Joe spent the rest of the night trailing Randy to rap clubs all over the city. Everywhere they went, fans screamed as soon as Randy entered. In one club Randy even got up on stage and performed "What U Do." Watching him rap, Frank had to agree Randy was hot.

He really could hold an audience with the edge that only a star could deliver.

It was three in the morning before Frank, Joe, and Randy got back to the hotel. Frank fell asleep the second his head hit the pillow. Randy Rand's lyrics were still echoing in his head.

Frank and Joe got a quick breakfast from room service the next morning. As soon as they'd eaten, showered, and dressed, the Hardys hurried out to find a cab. Joe hailed one in front of the Gramercy Hotel. They piled into the back, and Frank gave the cabbie the address of the studio where the Beastmaster rehearsed. Frank sat in silence on the way to the studio, thinking about the knife they'd found stuck in his pillow. Was Blue Lou really gunning for them? If so, did it mean they were getting close to an answer about who killed Martinelli?

"Earth to Frank," came Joe's voice. "What's with you?"

"Just thinking," Frank replied. "If Blue Lou did eliminate Martinelli, he'll probably start duping Randy's material himself. That could be a solid motive for him wanting Martinelli dead."

"Makes sense," Joe agreed. "I definitely wouldn't put murder past Blue Lou. Mobsters have a twisted sense of business etiquette. If they have a problem with someone, they simply get rid of him."

"And Martinelli was definitely a thorn in Chang's side," Frank added.

"If Chang is a counterfeiter, too," Joe reminded his brother. "We still don't know that for sure."

"True," Frank concluded. "Here's another 'if,' " he said. "It looks as if Chang and Martinelli were partners for a while. So why would Chang kill Martinelli now?"

Joe thought for a moment. The cab had turned onto Park Avenue and was heading uptown through the early-morning traffic.

"Maybe he saw the press conference and thought that would be an excellent chance to frame Randy," Joe suggested.

"But the medical examiner said it looked as though Martinelli was killed by the mob, execution style," Frank said. "If you were a mob hitman who wanted to pin the murder on an ordinary person, would you put a mob signature on it like that?"

Joe paused. "I guess mobsters just always do it the same way," he replied. "This case is starting to bug me. I hope we get something useful from Beastmaster J. I'm not convinced yet he wouldn't frame Randy. That guy acted totally unhinged when he barged into Randy's room."

"Randy was even more unhinged at the press conference, though," Frank replied.

The cab pulled over to the curb. Frank paid

the driver and glanced at the weathered building that matched the address Randy had given them.

"Randy said it was on the eighth floor," Frank said. "He also told me the elevator is usually broken."

Joe stared at the decrepit building. "I'm not surprised."

After seven flights of stairs, Frank and Joe stepped onto a landing and faced a plain door marked with stenciled lettering that read: BJ Studio.

"This must be the place," Frank said, opening the door.

The reception area was empty. Frank led the way farther into the studio. He stopped when he saw what appeared to be the engineering room. The Hardys peered through the small window on the door. Beastmaster J sat at a table, evidently mixing tracks. No engineer was with him, but Frank had heard of performers who preferred to mix their own material.

Beastmaster J's back was to them, and he had a pair of headphones on. Frank slowly opened the door. Joe was right behind him.

"Beastmaster?" Frank said.

The big man didn't reply. Frank figured the headphones were drowning out the sound of his voice. He walked up to the man and lightly tapped his shoulder.

Beastmaster J bolted up, ripping off his headphones and spinning around to face Frank and Joe.

"Are you crazy?" the Beastmaster shouted, his massive muscles bunching. "You don't ever sneak up on someone like that! What are you doing here?"

"I'm sorry," Frank apologized. "I didn't mean to surprise you. We're Frank and Joe Hardy—we met you with Randy Rand at his hotel. He's hired us to investigate Jack Martinelli's death to clear him. Could we ask you a few questions?"

Beastmaster J calmed down, smiling slightly. "Yeah, okay," he said softly. "I'll answer your questions. You guys don't seem like punks."

"Could you tell us where you were at the time of Martinelli's murder?" Joe asked, going for broke right at the start.

Beastmaster J put his hands up in the air. "Hey, look, Martinelli was a sleaze. Everyone knows that. But why would I want to mess with a dude like him? Besides, I was with another rapper, PJ Cool, when Martinelli was killed."

Joe opened his mouth to ask another question, but Frank interrupted him. "Just between us, Beastmaster, what is it between you and Randy?"

The rap star was surprised by the question. He rubbed his fist with his other hand and thought the question over. Finally he narrowed his eyes, stuck out his lower lip, and spoke.

"What is it?" Beastmaster J repeated. "I'll tell you what it is. Randy and I come from the same place—down. Now that we're both up, we should look out for each other, man, but Randy doesn't want it that way. He wants what he wants. It's okay. I'm my own man, he's his. I don't have to help him, and he doesn't need to help me."

"I don't get it. Why the bad blood?" Joe asked. "Did you guys ever have a fight?"

"Nope," Beastmaster said, shaking his head. "Never fought, just shouted." Finally he smiled. "I guess that's it, now that I think about it. Rapping is about who has the biggest mouth. I think that's what it is between us. Randy and I both want to have the biggest mouth." Beastmaster shrugged and held out his arms. "Of course, that's me. Randy just don't know it yet."

Frank laughed. He was starting to like the guy, even if he had a bad temper. "Thanks," he said, shaking the rap star's hand. "I think we found out all we needed to know."

Frank headed out of the studio, Joe in tow.

"What are you doing?" Joe asked, his face red with frustration. "I had more questions to ask that guy."

"It doesn't matter, Joe," Frank said, opening the front door of BJ Studio. "How could Beastmaster have committed the murder? The only ones who knew Martinelli's address were us and the police. Besides, I doubt he'd kill Martinelli just to frame Randy. He doesn't seem capable of it."

"I guess you're right," Joe said, automatically, pressing the button for the elevator. When he remembered it was broken, he held the door to the stairs open for Frank. "What about Blue Lou? I'm becoming more and more convinced of his guilt."

Frank and Joe headed down the stairs. "I guess we should head back. We promised to meet Randy for lunch," Frank said.

"We have to go back to the hotel anyway," Joe said. "I forgot my wallet."

"So, I guess the cab ride is on me again?" Frank said jokingly.

"I'll take care of lunch," Joe offered. "After I get my wallet."

Within fifteen minutes the Hardys were back at the Gramercy, heading for their room.

Frank opened the door and stood waiting while Joe picked his wallet up and shoved it in his back pocket. "Okay, we're ready," Joe announced.

Frank glanced at the desk and noticed a cassette recorder. "Hey, Joe. What's that?"

Joe reached the desk first and picked up a cassette and note. "It's from Randy," Joe said, reading the note, " 'Frank and Joe, this is a demo of my new song. I thought you might want to check it out. Randy.' "

Frank watched as Joe eagerly shoved the cassette into the recorder.

Joe hit Play, and Frank watched in horror as the recorder exploded, hurling Joe all the way across the room!

Chapter 10

THE EXPLOSION stunned Joe, and for a few seconds all he saw was bright light. When he came to, he found himself sprawled on the floor at the foot of his bed.

Frank rushed over to him. "Joe?" he cried out, checking his brother for injuries. "Are you okay?"

Joe blinked several times to get the soot out of his eyes. "Yeah," Joe said, grasping Frank's hand as Frank hauled him to his feet.

"Frank!" Joe cried, pointing to the bed.

Some schrapnel had landed on the sheets and the bed was smoldering.

"Quick," Frank said, tossing Joe a blanket from his bed. "We'll douse it."

Within seconds Frank and Joe had put out the small fire with blankets and towels and a pitcher of water dumped on for good measure. When it was over, Joe headed to the bathroom to wash his face, examining himself in the mirror. He had a nasty cut over his right eyebrow, which he cleaned before joining Frank in the room.

The older Hardy was by the desk, tinkering with the remains of the recorder. "Someone attached a crude explosive device to this," Frank explained. "Luckily, whoever did this was a real amateur."

"Who do you think did it, Frank? Did Randy plant the bomb?" Joe asked, touching the wound on his face.

"Randy would have to be pretty stupid to attempt this now," Frank said, still digging at the recorder with a pencil. "Also, why target us—we're on his side."

"Good point," Joe agreed. "But if not Randy, then who? Beastmaster J? Blue Lou? And whoever it was, how did the person get into our room?"

Joe went to the door and examined it. There was no sign of forced entry. He felt his frustration building. "Someone's out to get us, and it's obviously someone who can come in and out of our room as though it's his own. But who?"

Frank put the pencil aside and left the recorder on the desk. "Let's head over to Tight

Fist," he suggested. "We're supposed to meet Randy and Tabitha for lunch, remember."

Joe checked around for the note. He found a browned scrap of paper with a few letters still intact. "At least we have a clue this time," he said, tugging off his blackened shirt. "Not much is left, but there's enough to do a comparison. Give me a minute to clean up, and then we'll go."

Joe's brow ached slightly from the cut, but he counted himself fortunate. If a professional had engineered the bomb, he would have ended up incinerated like the note.

Joe followed Frank to Tabitha's office. Randy was standing outside the door, staring glumly at the floor. From inside the office, Joe could hear a man shouting, "You couldn't manage a lemonade stand, much less a recording studio!"

"What's up?" Joe asked Randy.

Randy raised his head to take in Frank and Joe. He smiled. "Tabitha's having a discussion with her father. He put up the money for Tight Fist, and I guess he isn't too hip to the press we've been getting lately."

"This is my business, Daddy!" Joe heard Tabitha shriek. "You gave it to me. It's mine. *Mine! Mine! Mine!*"

Joe looked at Frank, who was cringing. "Maybe we should call off lunch," he suggested.

Just then Tabitha poked her head out of the

office. "You're here? Fine. Listen, you guys go on without me," she said, her face livid.

She slammed the door, and her voice rose once more, "This is so unfair! You give me this business, then refuse to help me keep it alive!"

"You don't put cargo on a sinking ship, my dear," came the voice of Tabitha's father. "You abandon ship!"

"Let's go," Randy said, frustrated. "I can't take any more of this."

Joe and Frank followed Randy into the hall, where they spotted Mike Rigani and Keith Steiner, the sound engineers. The two men didn't seem to notice them, and Joe casually turned away.

"What's going on with Tabitha and her father?" Joe asked.

"Tabby's trying to get him to float her a loan," Randy replied, "until we can get this mess cleared up. The way I hear it, the old dude's not helping."

"They don't seem to get along very well," Frank added.

"It's from both sides, man," Randy said. "I mean, Mr. Cowan is a hard case. He's on her back all the time. I guess he just wants her to be successful. But Tabitha's got problems, too. I mean, I like Tabby, but she's the most spoiled person I've ever known. She's got a good business head, but she'll hold her breath until she turns blue if she doesn't get her way."

Randy glanced at Joe's face. "What happened to you, dude?"

"Just a little accident with a door," Joe replied.

"I know a great Middle Eastern place around the corner," Randy offered. "The Palm Café. Best falafel this side of Brooklyn. What do you say?"

"Sounds good to me," Joe replied, amazed at how well Randy was holding up. He had seemed like a wreck the previous night, but his spirits were pretty high now.

Ten minutes later Joe, Frank, and Randy were sitting at a round table right in front of a six-foot-high television screen that displayed music videos. Joe was surprised to see that the place was so hip. The Palm Café was packed, and Joe expected a mob of Randy's adoring fans to surround their table.

It never happened, though. Apparently Randy knew where he could eat without being bothered.

He also knew the spots with the best food. When his lamb kebabs came, Joe dug in. The three of them ate in silence. When they were done, they settled back and watched a few videos on the big-screen TV.

"So, what did you find out today?" Randy asked.

"The Beastmaster doesn't seem to be a solid suspect," Frank said. "He has an alibi and didn't have access to Martinelli's whereabouts.

We're focusing more on Blue Lou Chang. We definitely have a bone to pick with that guy."

"I'll say," Joe added.

"I didn't figure you'd get anything on the Beastmaster," Randy said. "I can't picture that dude killing anyone. It's not his style."

"So, have you had a chance to finish your demo tape?" Joe asked.

"I don't have one with all the tracks on it yet," Randy replied. "But as soon as I do, I'll hook you up with a copy."

"That'd be great," Joe said, sensing that Randy was telling the truth. It seemed more and more unlikely that he would have been the one to leave the bomb in their room.

"Listen, Randy," Frank cut in. "You really need to be straight with us about where you were the night Martinelli was killed."

"Hey, aren't you guys supposed to be helping me?" Randy said defensively. "I already told you, I was out walking."

"Where, Randy?" Frank continued. "I mean, put yourself in our shoes. Listen to your own story. How can we help you if you won't help yourself?"

"Listen, man. When I get mad, I just walk. That's how I cope. When my head is filled with rage, I walk until it's gone. I couldn't tell you exactly where I was. I was all over the East

Side, pounding the sidewalk. I couldn't even think straight, I was so mad."

"Did anyone see you?" Joe asked. "Did a fan come up and ask for your autograph or anything?"

"No," Randy replied. "I was walking with a major attitude, staring down at the pavement mostly. I didn't talk to anyone."

"Understand, Randy," Frank said, "we're not accusing you of anything. But if these other angles don't pan out, you'd better remember something, man. No matter how small or insignificant, you've got to try to remember a landmark, an incident, a person—anything to help us establish your alibi."

"I'll try," Randy muttered, his eyes on the tabletop.

Joe agreed with Frank's method. Randy needed to be aware of the possible consequences. Still, he hoped it wouldn't bring Randy too low to think about what might happen to him.

Joe glanced back to the television. A news anchor for the music television station was talking about rapper PJ Cool, who had left for a tour of Germany two days earlier.

Something about this bit of news struck Joe as strange. Then it hit him.

Beastmaster J couldn't have been with PJ Cool on the night of Martinelli's murder two days earlier, because PJ Cool was out of the country.

Beastmaster J had lied about his alibi!

Chapter 11

"FRANK!" JOE SHOUTED, jumping up from the table. "Did you hear that?"

"I sure did," Frank said, his eyes riveted on the screen.

"What's going on?" Randy asked, glancing back and forth between Joe and Frank.

"Beastmaster J lied about his alibi," Frank said. "He said he was with PJ Cool when Martinelli was killed. The news reporter just said that Cool's been on a tour in Germany."

Randy nodded slowly. "I could have told you guys that. They're having an anniversary celebration of the Berlin Wall coming down. I had a chance to go too, but I was too busy with my latest album."

"That means the Beastmaster just made it back on our suspect list," Joe said.

"I don't get it," Randy said. "Why would Beastmaster lie like that?"

"That's exactly what we're going to find out," Frank replied. "Come on, Joe," he said, quickly getting up from the table. "We're heading back to BJ Studio. We'll catch up with you later, Randy."

"I'll be at the hotel," Randy called after them. "Good luck, guys. And don't let the Beast bite you."

Within half an hour Frank and Joe were back at Beastmaster J's studios, making the grueling seven-story climb for the second time that day. At the top of the stairs, the Hardys were greeted by a locked door.

"Closed," Frank muttered. He pounded on the door for several seconds, but there was no answer.

"Maybe we should find a way in and look around," Joe suggested, reaching for his penknife.

"No way," Frank cautioned, noticing a maze of wires in the upper corner of the door. "This place has a serious alarm system. I don't know about you, but I'm not in the mood to explain anything to the police."

"So what now?" Joe asked anxiously.

"Back to the hotel, I guess," Frank replied.

"Let's ask Randy if he knows any of the Beastmaster's hangouts."

A few minutes later Frank and Joe's cab dropped them at the Gramercy. Pedro Torres was poised and waiting for them at their door.

"Pedro," Frank called out.

Torres turned around and smiled in their direction. "Hey, boys. I was just in the neighborhood and thought I'd drop in on you two. I hadn't heard from you in a while and figured you must have some leads by now."

"Let's go inside and talk," Joe suggested, unlocking the door.

As soon as they were inside, Torres noticed the burnt-out recorder on the desk. "What happened?" he asked.

"Bomb attempt," Frank answered.

Torres let out a low whistle.

"Jeez," he said. "I guess I was right. You do have some leads. In fact, it looks like your leads are too good. You're making someone very nervous."

"No kidding," said Joe, flopping down on his bed. "But whoever wired this recorder wasn't very experienced at it."

"This is the third attempt to scare us off," Frank said. "The first attempt was when a guy in a ski mask tried to push me in front of a subway train."

"The second attempt was a knife stuck in

Frank's pillow," Joe added. "A knife with a handle carved with the snake symbol from Chang's gang."

"So you think Blue Lou is behind all of this?" Torres asked.

"We did," Frank said, sitting on his bed, "until we questioned Beastmaster J. At first he had us pretty much convinced he was innocent. Then we found out he lied to us."

"I agree the Beastmaster is a solid suspect," Torres said. He grabbed a chair next to the desk, turned it around, and straddled it, his elbows resting on the back. "He could have street connections who told him where Martinelli was."

"That's true," Frank replied, "but I still say our number-one suspect is Blue Lou Chang. He even admitted to having us followed."

"You talked to him?" Torres asked.

"Sure," Joe replied. "We had to. The guy's a suspect."

"Don't mess with Blue Lou," Torres warned. "I'm going to follow up on him. I'm also going to try to track down the Beastmaster. For the time being, stay out of this. Let me take over now."

Joe was about to object, but Frank answered over him. "Sure, fine," he said.

"Good," Torres said. He got up and put the chair back by the desk. After giving the exploded bomb one last look, he warned the Hardys to be careful. "You don't know what you're messing with," he said. "No offense, but you kids may be out of your league."

With that, the detective left. Joe waited for the door to shut behind Torres before he exploded at Frank.

"What do you mean agreeing to stay off the case?" Joe demanded, his face bright red. "There's no way we're going to do that!"

"Of course we're not," Frank said with a huge grin. "So chill out. We started this, we're going to finish it. I have nothing against Torres, but I want to find the truth," Frank replied.

"It's the least we deserve," Joe said sullenly. "Especially since we were almost killed looking for it."

"Think of it this way," Frank said. "Now we have the NYPD sniffing around. It's nice to know they haven't written the whole thing off to Randy."

There was a knock at the door.

"Who is it?" Joe asked.

"It's Tabitha," came a reply from the hallway.

"Just a minute," Frank called back. He took a sheet from the bed and covered the recorder. "No reason to spread this around," he muttered to Joe.

Frank crossed the room and opened the door, ushering Tabitha into the room.

"Hi, guys," Tabitha said, her demeanor softened a bit. The record company owner was wearing a pair of tight black jeans and a black T-shirt. She pushed her blond hair behind her ears and smiled at Joe and Frank. "Sorry I skipped out on lunch."

"That's okay," Joe said. "We heard you talking with your father. Is everything okay?"

Tabitha shrugged. "Not really. But I don't want to bum you out talking about my father. I just wanted to check on how the investigation is going. I've been so busy we haven't had a chance to chat."

"We do have two strong suspects," Frank began. "Randy wasn't the only one with a motive. Beastmaster J could have had something to do with it. He's jealous of Randy and lied to us about his alibi. Framing Randy could put him on top again."

"We also suspect Blue Lou Chang," Joe added. "We think he was a rival counterfeiter whom Martinelli was competing with."

"Another counterfeiter?" Tabitha said with distaste. "They're all leeches. I can't stand them."

"We wouldn't have put him at the top of our list except that he had his gang follow us," Frank said.

"Not to mention the attempts someone's been making on us," Joe added.

"Attempts?" Tabitha asked, surprise crossing

her pretty face. "You don't mean, like, on your lives?" she said.

Frank frowned at Joe. "It's just someone trying to scare us away," Frank reassured her. "And we're pretty sure it's Blue Lou Chang."

"So, something's being done about it?" Tabitha asked.

"We talked to Detective Torres before you arrived," Joe replied. "He's going to question Chang, and he's also looking for the Beastmaster."

"Then maybe this whole mess will be over soon," Tabitha said. "I sure hope so. Tight Fist is already on such shaky ground."

"How so?" Frank asked.

Tabitha bit her lip, as if she regretted opening her mouth. "I just mean the bad publicity. Everything else is fine. Smooth sailing."

Frank had a feeling that something else was bothering Tabitha, but he didn't press it.

"That's good," Joe replied. "If we close this case, Tight Fist can finally reap some of the rewards it's due."

There was a knock on the door, followed by a thick voice announcing, "Room service."

Frank glanced at Joe. "Did you order anything?"

Joe shook his head.

Frank turned his attention to Tabitha. "Tabitha?"

"No," Tabitha replied. "I headed straight up. I didn't even stop at the front desk."

Frank checked with Joe. "I guess we'd better check it out."

Joe nodded. "You'd better stand back, Tabitha," Joe suggested.

"What's wrong?" Tabitha inquired, confused. "Room service probably just made a mistake."

"The way things have been going, I'm prepared for anything on the other side of that door," Frank said, stepping up to the door. He opened it slowly, Joe behind him.

A pushcart was in front of the door. A silver tray with a cover sat on the cart. The hallway was empty.

"What's that?" Joe asked. "Do you hear something?"

"Like a hissing sound, you mean?" Tabitha said, leaning toward them. "I think so."

Frank heard it, too. "Well, here goes. We might as well find out what it is."

He lifted the cover slowly. As soon as he did, Tabitha let out a scream.

Beneath the cover was a bright blue snake!

Chapter 12

FRANK STUMBLED BACK slightly, then realized that the snake was only a common garter snake painted blue. He quickly replaced the lid so it couldn't escape.

"Help!" Tabitha shouted.

"Calm down," Joe urged. He put an arm around Tabitha and pulled her back inside the room.

"I can't believe it," she said, breathing heavily into Joe's shoulder. "How could anyone do something like that?"

"It's just another friendly calling card," Joe grunted, his voice trembling with anger. "Courtesy of Blue Lou Chang. He painted a garter snake blue, so it resembled the symbol of his gang, and had it delivered to our room."

"What is it with this guy? Why is he going after you like this?" Tabitha asked, pulling free of Joe's arm.

"I don't know, but I've had it with him," Joe said. He was sorry to lose Tabitha from his embrace, but knew he'd better concentrate on the case. "I say it's time we pay him another visit."

"You're right," Frank agreed. "We have to confront him and stop all of this before it gets out of hand."

"Are you sure you should go back there?" Tabitha asked. "Maybe you should just let the police take care of it."

"No way," Joe replied. "If he wants to try something, let him try it face-to-face."

"I think we should head over there just to talk, Joe," Frank said. "Try to find out why he's coming down so heavy on us. Let him know that Sam Peterson is a good friend of ours."

"Whatever," Joe muttered, picturing the hurt he was going to deliver to Blue Lou. Maybe Frank was scared of the guy, but he wasn't.

"Tabitha," Frank said, "you'd better head out now."

"What about the snake?" she asked, her eyes still wide with alarm.

"Could you take it to a pet store, or maybe the animal shelter?" Joe asked.

Tabitha's shoulders sagged. "Not on your life. I'm not getting near that thing. I'll call down to the desk," she said, crossing the room. "Let them deal with it. They were the ones who let someone in with it."

Tabitha reached for the phone and dialed down to the desk. Within a few minutes she had arranged for a bellboy to come up with a bag to take the snake away.

"You guys can go ahead," Tabitha told them with a grim smile. "I'll wait for the bellboy."

"You sure you'll be okay?" Joe asked.

"Fine," Tabitha replied. She glanced over at the room service cart. "I just hope he doesn't get any slimy ideas!" she joked.

Frank and Joe made their way to the elevator laughing. As they headed outside, Joe's mind was racing. "I can't wait to confront Blue Lou," he said as Frank hailed a cab.

"I have to admit, he sure is making this case easy for us," Frank said, after he gave the cab driver the address for Chang's warehouse.

"Yeah," Joe said. "If he wanted to convince us he was innocent of Martinelli's murder, he wouldn't have pulled these stunts."

"Maybe it's pride with him," Frank offered. "Maybe he doesn't like us being so close to his operations. Still, a legitimate businessman wouldn't send a snake on a silver platter to someone."

"I don't care what his problem is," Joe replied sternly. "I don't care if it has to do with

Martinelli's murder or his counterfeiting enterprise or whatever. Blue Lou is going to come clean with us."

"We have to be careful, Joe," Frank said. "As upset as you are, you have to keep in mind what sort of man Blue Lou is. He commands a lot of power. We're going there to try to put a stop to his threats, but we need to do it in a civilized and nonviolent way."

"Sure thing, Frank," Joe said. "You have your civilized ways, and I have mine."

Frank let out a long sigh. "Just try to keep your temper, okay?"

"Okay," Joe said glumly.

No one was posted in front of Chang's warehouse as the cab pulled to a stop at the curb. Was Chang expecting them? Joe wondered if they might be walking into a trap. He was keenly aware of every little sound. The last thing he and Frank needed was to find themselves in an ambush.

"Keep on your guard," Frank muttered as he and Joe entered the warehouse. It was quiet—too quiet for a place of business. The warehouse was no longer empty—crates and boxes were stacked on the main floor, Frank noted.

"It's midafternoon," Joe said. "There should be people in here working, especially since merchandise is back on the floor."

"Look at this, Joe," Frank said, motioning to

a small box propped up on a crate. It contained printed covers for Randy's latest CD.

"Now that Martinelli's out of the way, it definitely looks like Chang is going ahead with duping CDs," said Joe.

"Let's wait until all of the facts are in," Frank replied. "Chang might be duping CDs and tapes, taking advantage of Martinelli's death. That doesn't necessarily mean he's guilty of murder.

"I don't like this, Joe," Frank said after a moment. "How do we know Chang's men haven't let him know we were on our way here? This whole thing feels like a trap."

"I know," Joe replied. "But we've come too far to stop now."

Joe and Frank took the stairs up one flight to Chang's office. Joe took a deep breath, turned the knob, and pushed the door in.

Blue Lou Chang sat on his sofa, seemingly waiting patiently for them. "Come in, my young friends," Chang said, smiling. "What a pleasant surprise."

"Now, listen," Frank said as he and Joe entered Chang's office. "We're not here to cause trouble. We just wanted you to know that Chief of Police Sam Peterson is a close friend of ours, and he won't appreciate all of the threats you've been throwing at us."

"Again!" Blue Lou exclaimed, standing up. "This is the third time you've barged in on me, you amateurs. Haven't you learned anything from my messages?"

Joe couldn't stand it any longer. He grabbed Blue Lou by the lapels of his jacket.

"I'm tired of being kicked around by you!" Joe shouted in his face.

Frank grasped Joe's arms from behind, but Joe maintained his hold, relishing the horror on Chang's face. "The knife and snake were cute, but the subway attempt and the exploding recorder are just a little more than you can expect us to take, pal! Now talk, or I'll plaster you to your wall!"

"Let go, Joe!" Frank demanded, pinning Joe's arms and pulling him away from Blue Lou.

Blue Lou adjusted his glasses and smoothed out his jacket. "What are you talking about?" he demanded. "Yes, I have had you followed. Yes, I left warnings for you. But I did not intend for anyone to hurt you. I wanted you to mind your own business. Which you still seem unable to do."

"So, you expect us to believe that you had nothing to do with that exploding recorder?" Joe asked while Frank still held him from behind.

"That is exactly what I expect you to believe," Chang replied. "I have no knowledge of any such incident."

"Okay," Frank said, relaxing his hold on Joe.

"Let's everyone just relax before someone gets hurt."

Chang shook his head apologetically. "Hurting people is not my style. Especially people who have done no wrong to me. You've crossed that line today, Joe Hardy, and for that there is a price you and your brother must pay!"

Chang snapped his fingers. The office door burst open. Joe and Frank whirled around to see four gang members dressed in ninja outfits. Each of them carried illegal martial arts weapons—nunchucks, throwing stars, and broad swords.

"Kill them!" Joe heard Chang shout from behind him!

Joe felt helpless with horror as the four gang members approached them, their weapons ready.

Chapter 13

"So, WHOSE bright idea was it to come here anyway?" Joe asked, backing up slightly as the gang members circled him and Frank.

While Frank sized up the opposition, he was also looking for potential weaknesses. He didn't see any. "I'll take the guys with the sword and stars," Frank whispered. "Get in close, try to disarm them quick. I'll try to give you a hand—"

That was the last thing Frank was able to say before the four ninjas charged. Frank stepped up and planted himself firmly. The man with the broadsword swung at him. Frank sidestepped the blade and wrapped his arm around the man's forearm.

Still holding the guy, Frank jabbed him in the

nose and took his weapon away. Frank felt a sudden pain in his shoulder. He turned to see the guy with the nunchucks getting ready to administer another blow.

Frank swiped at the man's face with the sword handle, which he followed up with sweeping at the guy's legs, backing him up. Frank punched the fallen man in the chest, then looked up.

Joe was pinned against the wall by the two other assailants. Both men were throwing punches into Joe's abdomen. Frank raced over, throwing a round kick against the side of one man's head. The other one got a blow to his chest from Frank's tightened fist.

Joe slumped to the floor, and Frank took the chance to kneel down to check on his brother. It was a bad move, Frank realized as he felt something strike him from behind. Frank fell to the floor and his vision clouded as a sharp pain exploded at the base of his skull.

"Now," Frank heard Chang say through the veil over his senses. "Kill them!"

"Freeze!" Frank heard a booming voice shout.

Frank was just able to focus on Pedro Torres standing in the office doorway. The detective was backed by several uniforms. All of the officers had their weapons trained on the assailants.

"Drop your weapons! Now!" Torres barked.

Frank heard the sound of the martial arts

weapons falling to the floor. He crawled over to Joe, who was gently rubbing his ribs.

"Are you okay?" Frank asked him.

Joe nodded. "Nothing broken. How about you?"

"I'll live," Frank said, lightly touching the back of his head.

"I should have known you two wouldn't listen to me," Torres said, standing over the Hardys. "I'd better call for an ambulance."

"No need," Frank said, standing up and helping Joe to his feet. "We're a little bruised, but okay."

"You're sure you don't need a doctor to look at you?" Torres asked.

"I'm sure," Joe said. "We've taken worse."

Frank glanced at Chang, who was facing the wall as an officer frisked him. "We found labels for Randy's CD in a box in the warehouse," Frank informed Torres. "I think he was going to take over where Martinelli left off."

"I know," Torres replied. "I've got my men confiscating all the material in the warehouse. Chang was counterfeiting every artist Tight Fist represented. We have the proof downstairs."

"That's why he wanted us out of his hair," Frank said. "It also explains why the warehouse had been cleared out yesterday—they needed the space for the CDs and tapes." He was starting to feel a little better. The pounding at the back of his head had dulled to a low throb.

"You can also see how it would be to his advantage to have Martinelli out of the way," Joe added.

"I didn't kill anyone!" Chang protested from across the room.

"I really believe that," Torres shot back. "Especially the way your punks were attacking my friends here. You should be grateful they weren't hurt. Then you'd have a real problem."

"They attacked me!" Chang shouted. "I was merely defending myself! I'm going to press charges against them!"

"Mr. Chang, you have the right to remain silent. Use it," Torres advised. The detective turned back to the Hardys. "We have a lot to nail him for. Illegal weapons and counterfeiting. Attempted murder."

Frank nodded. "I guess we owe you one," he said ruefully. "You saved our lives."

Torres waved his hand across his face. "It was nothing," he said. "I'm still waiting for that autograph, though."

The police officers led Blue Lou Chang away in handcuffs. Joe gave Chang a huge grin as he left his office. "See ya. Glad I'm not you!"

"You just couldn't resist one parting shot, could you?" Frank said, chuckling.

"I should get some satisfaction out of this. Right?" Joe said, cradling his ribs. "I guess there's something about being nearly killed that brings out my sarcastic side."

Joe made a quick call to find Randy. "I want to let him know about Blue Lou," he told Frank. At Tight Fist, the receptionist informed him that Randy was on his way to the studio to rehearse.

"If we catch a cab, we might get there the same time he does," Joe suggested.

Joe and Frank said a quick goodbye to Torres and hopped in a cab. When they arrived at Tight Fist, Bonnie informed them that they had just missed Randy, who was in one of the sound studios. Joe and Frank rushed down the hallway and into the studio, where Randy was sitting alone in front of a synthesizer.

"Hey, dudes!" Randy said good-naturedly. "You caught me getting ready to lay down a couple of tracks."

"We have good news for you," Frank said. "Blue Lou Chang was just taken into police custody on several charges. They might even investigate him for Martinelli's murder."

"That's great," Randy exclaimed. "Are you telling me I'm cleared?"

"Not yet," Joe replied. "There hasn't been a formal charge made against Chang for Martinelli's murder, but he's definitely in the running for prime suspect."

"I can't thank you guys enough," Randy said, relieved. "You really pulled through for me."

"Thank us when it's over," Frank added. "I don't think any prosecutor would disregard all the evidence pointing to Chang, but I'm not getting my hopes up, either."

"Do you guys think he did it?" Randy asked.

"Considering the number of threats he made against us and the gang he ordered to kill us, I wouldn't be surprised," Frank replied.

"Whoa," Randy said. "Did I miss something?"

"Only the fight of the century between us and four of Chang's gang members," Joe retorted. "Lucky for us, though, that Detective Torres showed up with his men."

"Are you dudes okay?" Randy asked, concerned.

"Just a couple of aches and pains," Frank reassured him. "Nothing a nice hot shower won't cure."

"I'm glad to hear that," Randy said.

Frank glanced over at Joe, who was eyeing a microphone positioned in front of a guitar.

"You know," Joe said, "I've always wanted to see what it would feel like to sing in a real live recording studio."

Frank rolled his eyes. "I don't believe you," he said. "We've just been in the fight of our lives, and you decide you want to try a new career as a singer!"

"Maybe that's why," Joe said with a huge grin. "Maybe I just realized how dangerous our chosen profession really is. Seriously, the case is wrapping up—why not cut loose? Randy?"

Randy shrugged. "It's the least I can do for you, man."

Randy pulled a stool up for Joe to sit on. "Here. Put these headphones on, sit here, and then sing into the microphone," the rap star told Joe. "The control room is upstairs for this studio, so we'll go up and cue up some music for you.

"Come on," Randy said to Frank. "Let's go up and watch our future star through the window."

Frank followed Randy out of the rehearsal studio and up a flight of stairs to the engineer's room. Once they entered the darkened room, Randy relieved the engineer at the console.

"We'll take it from here, dude," Randy said, perching at the console after the man left. "Have a seat," Randy said to Frank, patting the chair next to his. "You can help me out with the controls."

"Actually, I know a thing or two about this," Frank said.

"Really? Cool," Randy replied. "Then we can make a hit record for your brother." Randy laughed out loud. "Who knows? Maybe the guy's got what it takes to go platinum. You can retire and count your money on the beach in Barbados."

"Wait until you hear him sing first," Frank

warned, glancing down into the recording booth. Joe seemed to be beckoning to him. When Frank squinted, he realized Joe's expression was one of horror.

Joe Hardy was pounding against the studio door now, his mouth open in a silent scream!

Chapter 14

"COME ON, RANDY!" Frank shouted, jumping up from behind the console. "Joe's in trouble!"

Frank rushed back down the stairs and saw that a chair had been shoved under the rehearsal booth doorknob. He could hear Joe pounding on the door.

Frank removed the chair and opened the door. Joe spilled out, clutching his throat and gasping for fresh air.

"Keep back," Joe wheezed, bending over and catching his breath. "There's gas in there. Ammonia mixed with bleach from what I can tell."

"What happened?" Randy asked.

"I was sitting there when I heard a sound like glass breaking," Joe said, catching his breath.

"When I turned around, I watched the door being closed and noticed a broken jar on the floor. Then the place started filling with fumes. I tried the door, but someone had locked it."

"Did you see anyone?" Frank asked.

"No," Joe said, glancing down the hallway beyond Frank to a rear exit by the stairway. "But that must be how he got out of here. Might be how he came in, too."

"We should get out of this hall," Randy replied. "That stuff is rank."

"Prop open the exit," Joe suggested. "Let's get some fresh air in the building."

"Who could have done this?" Frank wondered. "I mean, Chang is in jail."

Joe shook his head, standing upright. His head still swam a little, but it was clearing. He knew one thing, though. Randy hadn't been the one. He had been with Frank the whole time. Joe was positive now that Randy was innocent.

"We should pay a surprise visit to Beastmaster J," Frank said. "He's our only other suspect."

Joe nodded. "Yeah, whoever did that might have been expecting to find Randy in that room."

"What?" Randy said in disbelief. "You think someone was trying to kill me?"

"Looks that way," Joe replied. "Anyone who opened the door and tossed the jar would have no idea I was in there. They'd assume it was you. I think someone was gunning for you."

"This is so uncool," Randy complained. "I mean, I'm accused of murder, then someone tries to nail me?"

"It's just a theory," Frank interjected. "It could have been one of Chang's men trying to get back at us. Either way, we're on it. Don't worry."

"I'll try not to," Randy agreed. "You sure you're okay, Joe? I never thought—man . . ." For once, Randy was completely speechless.

"It's okay, Randy," Joe assured him. "This kind of thing comes with the territory. I was kind of hoping to try a little singing, but what the hey. Look—can you tell us where we might find Beastmaster J?" Joe asked. "We tried his studio, but it was closed."

"He has a room at a place near the Gramercy. I think it's called the City Arms," Randy said.

"We'll go question him," Frank said. "Why don't you head back to your room and stay put? If someone was after you just now, you could be in danger still. Joe and I'll find you after we question the Beastmaster."

"You got it," Randy replied.

Less than half an hour later Joe and Frank were standing in front of the City Arms Hotel, a few blocks from the Gramercy Hotel. As soon as they walked into the lobby, they saw Beastmaster J step into the elevator.

"Come on," Joe said, hurriedly making his way to the elevator. He stuck his arm inside, blocking the doors and forcing them open.

"Beastmaster," Frank said. "We have to talk."

"I've told you guys everything I know," the Beastmaster insisted.

"PJ Cool was in Germany the night of Martinelli's murder," Joe replied.

Beastmaster J stared uneasily at the Hardys. "Let's go to my room," he said finally. "I'll explain everything there."

The Hardys followed the Beastmaster to his unkempt room. Clothes and papers were strewn all over the place, and it looked like a maid hadn't come around in weeks.

"I went to a movie alone the night of the murder," the Beastmaster said, sitting on the edge of his bed. "Right after the press conference. I knew it was the lamest alibi in the world, and I also knew that PJ would back me. We're tight. I just forgot what day he left on his tour."

"That leaves you unaccounted for during Martinelli's murder," Frank said.

"Yeah, but I didn't kill him, okay? I'd never hurt anyone," the Beastmaster vowed. "Not even Randy Rand."

"We've been attacked several times these last few days, most recently earlier this afternoon at

Tight Fist. Do you have alibis for those times?" Frank asked.

"Look," the Beastmaster said finally. "I haven't been trying to hurt you. I've got nothing else to say to you, okay? If you want to turn me over to the cops, fine. But I'm not wasting my breath on you anymore. So just go."

"Thanks for your time," Joe said as he and Frank left the Beastmaster's room.

"What do you think?" Joe asked Frank as they headed into the elevator.

"I think the Beastmaster may be hiding something," Frank replied, pushing the Down button on the control panel. "I don't care who you are. You don't lie about your alibi if you're innocent."

"Maybe he was just genuinely scared," Joe suggested. "Maybe he knows he's an immediate suspect because of his and Randy's ongoing feud."

"Do you think he killed Martinelli?" Frank asked.

"Not really," Joe admitted. "But someone's up to something, someone other than Chang. I don't think he'd be stupid enough to retaliate now, in the midst of all of his problems. I'm sure we're the last thing on his mind."

"Then that leaves Randy, and I don't think he'd plot the murder of someone who had just cleared him of a crime," Frank pointed out. "Actually, I was with him the whole time, and he couldn't have thrown the bottle of bleach and ammonia."

"There's an unknown person working here, Frank," Joe said, stepping out of the elevator as the doors opened.

"What do you mean?" Frank asked.

"We've got a loose cannon out there. We'd better find our suspect fast. Real fast."

Joe and Frank were still tossing possibilities at each other in the lobby of the Gramercy Hotel. "What about Mr. Cowan?" Joe suggested. "Maybe he wants Tabitha to fail."

"You're grasping, Joe," Frank replied. "Why would a successful man like Cowan try to sabotage his own daughter's career? Besides, why would he have murdered Martinelli?"

"Just checking for other possibilities," Joe said as he and Frank rode to the fourth floor.

"The only good thing about this business is, when you least expect it, a clue usually jumps right out at you," Frank said.

They stepped into the hallway, heading for Randy's room. Before they reached his door, they could hear a familiar voice shouting from inside the room.

"Randy Rand, I'm going to kill you!"

Frank and Joe exchanged a look of total surprise. Tabitha Cowan was threatening to kill her number-one act.

Chapter 15

FRANK WATCHED as Tabitha stormed out of Randy's room and marched past them, an expression of outrage on her face. She didn't even bother to stop and look at either him or Joe.

Frank turned back to Randy's door, where Randy was standing on the threshold, shaking his head grimly.

"What was that all about?" Joe asked him.

Randy held up a check. "I can't cash my royalty check because Tight Fist doesn't have enough money in the bank," Randy reported. "Tabitha's telling me that business has been down and that the setback is only temporary. She said I'll have my cash soon."

"So what's the problem?" Frank asked.

"Tabitha can tell me to wait all she wants, but I can't afford to stay with Tight Fist," Randy replied, shoving the check into his pocket. "I'm going to be a major star after the Garden show. I've even gotten a few offers already. I told Tabitha that unless she can put some money behind me, I'll have to get a bigger label to handle me. One that can cover my checks."

"Aren't you being a little rash?" Frank asked. "I mean, after all you've been through, things are sure to smooth out now."

"Hey, man," Randy said, slightly offended. "I wouldn't dump on Tabitha for no good reason. Bottom line is, Tight Fist is going down fast and I'm abandoning ship before it sinks." With that, Randy stepped back into his room. "Hate to be rude, dudes, but I'm zonked. Check with you in the morning, okay?"

"Sure," said Joe as Randy closed his door.

Frank glanced at his watch and noted that the evening had grown long. "I say we call room service for a sandwich and hit the sack ourselves," he suggested to Joe. "We'll come up with a game plan in the morning."

Frank and Joe rose early the next morning, both anxious to plot out their day. With Chang in custody, there was the question of who had tried to gas Joe—or Randy, if it had been meant for him. Frank put in a quick call to Torres and learned that Chang was still denying the fact that he had made any attempts on their lives, including the explosive recorder. He also claimed not to be involved in Martinelli's murder.

"That leaves at least three loose ends," Frank said, hanging up the phone. "The recorder, the gas in the studio—"

"And the biggest one of all," Joe said, finishing off his cereal. "Who killed Martinelli? And is that person going to keep coming after us?"

Frank shook his head, still deep in thought. "You know, I didn't like the tone of Tabitha's voice," Frank said. "It made me nervous seeing her that upset."

"You have to admit, though. She had good reason to be upset," Joe replied.

"But you don't threaten to kill someone," Frank said. "After that outburst, I'd say that Tabitha may deserve our consideration in this case."

"She was at Tight Fist when the murder took place," Joe reminded Frank. "How could she have been involved?"

"I don't know," Frank admitted. "But let's look at her from a psychological point of view. She's from a wealthy family. This business is evidently a test her father has set up for her. Tabitha is Mr. Cowan's only heir. You heard yourself how demanding he was."

"A perfectionist," Joe agreed. "And he wants Tabitha to be one, too."

"Right. Doesn't it all add up to the fact that Tabitha has a lot to lose if Tight Fist folds?" Frank submitted.

"Yeah, but do you think she'd turn to murder to save face?" Joe said.

Frank shrugged. "I'm not sure. We know Tabitha Cowan is used to having her way. We also know she totally despised Martinelli for what he was doing. She has a big temper—we heard her threaten Randy."

"We still don't have any hard evidence, Frank," Joe said. "And we still can't put her at the murder site. Martinelli hadn't been dead for long when we found him. Tabitha couldn't have beat us there."

"I didn't say she murdered Martinelli," Frank said. "I'm just saying she deserves our consideration."

"I'm not sure what to make of all this," Joe muttered.

"Tabitha has motive. Martinelli was ruining her company," Frank pointed out.

"But Martinelli had been arrested," Joe said. "His material had been confiscated."

"Also, at the press conference, Tabitha heard Torres tell us that Martinelli would probably reopen shop," Frank replied.

"How did she get his address?" Joe said.

"Only you and I and the police knew that. Randy only knew that Martinelli operated out of Queens."

"I guess you're right," Frank said. "Well, we still have Beastmaster J to consider. He had a lot to gain by framing Randy."

"Which brings us back to Tabitha," Joe interjected. "Would she have tried to frame Randy, her top star? Or would she have tried to kill him with a combination of ammonia and bleach fumes?"

"The Tight Fist pin smelled like a plant," Frank replied. "Still, it could have been dropped accidentally."

"It doesn't make sense to me," Joe complained. "I mean, I can see your point about how Tabitha must have hated Martinelli. I just don't see how she could have pulled it off. Out of all our suspects, she's the only one with a rock-solid alibi."

"Randy was out walking the streets," Frank recalled. "Beastmaster J was seeing a movie. Chang, our most obvious suspect, is unaccounted for, but he's still our most likely suspect. And then there's Tabitha. We left her at Tight Fist before we headed over to Martinelli's."

"I'd be willing to pin the whole thing on Chang if that stunt at the studio hadn't happened," Joe said.

"Someone was really sloppy," Frank agreed.

"We had a suspect behind bars and someone still tried to take one of us out."

"Or Randy," Joe reminded him. "Although I still don't get why the real killer would try to hurt Randy."

"If Randy were found guilty, the killer could rest easy," Frank agreed.

"If the police let Chang go because of a lack of evidence, Randy would be the number-one suspect again," Joe realized. "So why would Chang have an attempt made on Randy's life?"

A swift knock on the door cut short their discussion. Frank rose and answered it.

Randy stood in the doorway. "Hey, dudes," he said, smiling weakly.

Frank noticed a recorder in Randy's hand.

"I have that demo tape you guys were asking about," he said, walking over to the desk and setting the recorder down. "Want to hear it?"

"You bet," Joe said eagerly.

Frank was curious himself. "I'd love to."

"I meant to play it for you last night," Randy said, putting a cassette into the recorder. "But that scene with Tabitha was a major downer and I totally forgot I had this for you. Check it out."

Frank exchanged an excited glance with Joe. Randy Rand was going to play a new song for them! Although he hadn't started out as a Randy Rand fan when the case began, Frank had to admit that he had really come to like the rapper's music.

Randy hit the Play button. The song began, and Randy's sharp voice blasted out of the recorder.

"Think with your heart / not with your mind / go on a soul search / see what you find / banish the pain now / leave it behind . . ."

Frank and Joe applauded as the last notes died down. Just before Randy hit the Stop button, Frank thought he heard a strange sound coming from the tape recorder, one that wasn't music at all.

"Did you guys hear that?" Frank said. "It sounded like someone's voice or something."

"I didn't hear anything," Joe said.

"This is just a rough mix. There could be some sounds from the studio on here," Randy said.

"Do you mind if we hear it again?" Frank asked, reaching for the Rewind button.

"Go ahead," Randy said.

Frank rewound the tape for a few seconds, then hit Play. The last notes of the song played again, and this time Frank could clearly make out a voice.

" . . . warehouse in Queens," the voice said.

Frank was astonished. It was Joe's voice, giving the location of Martinelli's warehouse!

Chapter 16

"HOW DID THAT get on there?" Frank asked excitedly, pointing to the recorder.

"Oh," Randy said casually, hitting the Stop button. "I guess the engineer must have left a mike on and the tape running when Joe was telling me about Martinelli's arrest. But it's cool. We can edit it out during the mixing process."

"Oh, I see," Joe said, glancing at Frank knowingly. "Well, the song was great, Randy. Frank and I have some business to see to, so—"

"I'm out of here," Randy said. "I don't want to stand in the way of justice." Randy pulled two tickets out of his shirt pocket. "That's whack, man. I almost forgot to give you guys these backstage passes to the show at the Garden tonight."

Joe's eyes went wide as he took them from Randy. "Wow!" he said. "Backstage at the Garden. Thanks, man. I just thought we'd be in the audience."

"I want to see you guys there tonight," Randy said. "The Power Brokers and Randy Rand will rock New York City."

Randy gave Frank and Joe each a low five, picked up the recorder, and left the room.

"You know what this means?" Frank said after Randy was gone.

"Yeah," Joe replied. "Tabitha has complete access to Randy's tapes. She could have heard the part about Martinelli's warehouse."

"But we haven't proven anything," Frank said, perplexed.

"Let's go see Mr. Cowan," Joe suggested. "Maybe he can shed some light on Tight Fist and just how far Tabitha might go to keep it. After all, who should know Tabitha Cowan better than her own father?"

Joe and Frank easily found Cowan's office, which was located near Wall Street. They'd rummaged some ties out of their bags, and looked fairly presentable when they showed up at his receptionist's desk an hour later.

"We need to speak with Mr. Cowan," Frank

said to the young woman, who immediately glanced down at an appointment book.

"Is he expecting you?" she asked.

"No," Joe replied. "But we're sure he won't mind talking to us. Our father is interested in making large financial investments in some of Mr. Cowan's franchises."

"Well, Mr. Cowan normally sees people only by appointment," the woman insisted.

"That's too bad," Frank said, leaning close. "You see, we'll only be in town for the day and we're talking multimillion-dollar transactions. I don't think Mr. Cowan will be happy if you turn us away."

"What are your names?" the woman asked, blushing slightly.

"Joe and Frank Hardy," Joe replied.

The receptionist picked up the phone receiver and spoke into it. After a few seconds she quietly hung the phone up and smiled at the Hardys. "Mr. Cowan says you can go right in."

Joe and Frank stepped into Cowan's office, which was spacious but modestly furnished with a wooden desk and straight-backed chairs. Cowan, a balding, slightly overweight man, greeted the Hardys.

"Mr. Cowan," Joe said, extending his hand. "I'm Joe Hardy and this is my brother, Frank."

"The pleasure is mine," Cowan said, shaking the Hardys' hands. "Please, have a seat."

"We appreciate your seeing us on such short notice," Frank said as he and Joe sat down.

"No problem. I had a slight lull between conference calls," Cowan said, perching on the edge of his desk. "So, Susan tells me that your father is interested in buying into the business?"

"Yes," Joe said. "Our father, Fenton Hardy, has a large security network. He handles everything. Personal protection. Alarm systems. Even industrial undercover work."

"Did he have a specific venture in mind?" Cowan asked.

"Yes," Frank replied. "Tight Fist Records."

Cowan's friendly face suddenly tensed. "I'm afraid you've come to the wrong place. My company is in no way affiliated with Tight Fist. In fact, I'm sure my daughter's pitiful venture will soon fail."

"Is there a reason for you to think so?" Frank asked. He took out a pad of paper he carried in the inside breast pocket of his jacket and pretended to look something up there. "According to the figures my father gave us, the business is doing okay, though not fantastically well."

Cowan coughed. "You can tell your father that as of this moment I'm not entirely pleased with my daughter or her business judgment. I just found out that she's been making large cash withdrawals from the company. I think you'd better tell your father to hold on to his money."

At that moment the man's phone rang. Cowan held up his hand in apology and answered it. After a few seconds he placed his hand over the receiver and said to Frank and Joe, "I'm afraid I have to take this call. If you wouldn't mind waiting outside, I'll be just a few minutes."

Frank smiled and stood up. "No problem," he said, walking toward the door with Joe right behind him.

Once the Hardys were back in the reception area, Frank and Joe exchanged a look. "I think we got what we needed," Frank said to his brother. "What do you think?"

Joe nodded. "Let's go before he comes back out and asks to check our credentials," he said, his voice low just in case the receptionist was listening.

Frank and Joe thanked the receptionist and told her to inform Mr. Cowan that they had to leave. "We just remembered another appointment we have uptown," he told her. "We'll be in touch."

With that, the Hardys left Cowan's building. Once they were outside, Frank turned to his brother and asked, "Why do you think Tabitha's been making large withdrawals? Tight Fist can't even cover a royalty check for Randy."

"Maybe she was buying stuff for herself," Joe suggested. "Remember her office?"

"I don't think she'd run the business into the

ground for a new wardrobe," Frank replied. "So what is she doing with that money?"

"I don't know," Joe said. "Whatever it is, it seems pretty suspicious."

"The problem is, we probably won't get a chance to question her this afternoon," Frank said. "Not with Randy's show taking place tonight."

Frank found a phone booth and tried calling Tight Fist. Once he got through, his worst suspicions were confirmed. Tabitha was, according to the receptionist, unavailable. Frank hung up, frustrated.

"No luck?" Joe asked.

"Zero," Frank confirmed.

Suddenly Joe's face brightened. "I know. We can question her tonight at the Garden," Joe suggested. "We'll be backstage. And we know she'll have to be there. Piece of cake. I still don't think she's the one we're looking for, for the record."

Frank thought for a moment. "I guess that's all we can do—wait until tonight."

Frank and Joe grabbed lunch, then headed back to the hotel, where they each took a nap. After showering and getting dressed, Frank and Joe had a quick dinner in the hotel restaurant.

It was early, but Joe wanted to head to the Garden, anyway. "We can watch them set up," he told Frank as they stood waiting for a cab.

At the Garden they had to work their way through the mob of fans to a side entrance, where a huge bodyguard ushered them inside after checking their passes.

Joe and Frank stood out of the way on the ramp backstage. People were all over the place. Lighting men. Sound engineers. Dozens of workers moving at breakneck speed to prepare for the thousands of people Joe knew would be filling the space.

Tabitha brushed past Frank and Joe and approached Mike Rigani and Keith Steiner, the two sound engineers from Tight Fist.

Joe nudged Frank, and the two Hardys moved within earshot of the trio. Frank kept his eyes on Tabitha, watching for any suspicious moves. He wanted to question her, but knew he had to think about the right approach. Mike and Keith were checking equipment. Mike wore a Tight Fist button. Keith didn't.

"What happened to your pin?" Tabitha asked Keith, pointing at his sleeveless vest.

"I must have lost it," Keith replied.

Tabitha reached into her pocketbook and pulled out another pin. "Here," she said. "Try to take better care of this one."

Frank watched as a man approached Tabitha with a clipboard.

"I need a signature for some of this equipment, Ms. Cowan," the man said.

Tabitha frowned. "I just had my nails done. Sign it for me, would you, Keith?"

Keith took a pen from the man and scribbled on the clipboard. At that same moment, someone bumped into Frank from behind and he practically fell on top of the delivery man. The clipboard fell to the floor. Frank picked it up and found himself staring hard at Keith's signature.

"Sorry," Frank said, handing the clipboard back.

Something clicked in Frank's head. Something about the handwriting. Frank stepped aside and quickly took the remainder of the note Joe had found taped on the exploding recorder and studied it.

The handwriting seemed to be the same.

"What was that all about?" Joe asked.

"Come on, Joe," Frank whispered, tugging his brother away.

Joe and Frank retreated farther backstage, where there weren't so many people around. "Tabitha may have an alibi, but that doesn't mean she didn't hire someone to kill Martinelli," Frank explained. "I heard Keith say he lost his pin. What if he lost it at Martinelli's warehouse?"

"That's pretty circumstantial evidence, Frank," Joe said.

"I know," Frank went on, his heart beating triple time. "Except that I just saw Keith sign for something and his handwriting matches that on our note."

"That means Chang was telling the truth about not wanting to hurt us," Joe added. "Tabitha must have had her hired help try to take us out."

"We've got to find a phone," Frank said, glancing along the length of the wall for a pay phone.

Without warning Frank felt something cold and hard press into the small of his back. Someone had the barrel of a gun dug into his spine!

Chapter 17

JOE GLANCED OVER at Frank and saw Mike Rigani pressed up close behind his brother.

"That must be you behind me, Keith," Joe said, assuming that Rigani had a gun trained on Frank as well.

"Smart boy." Keith chuckled. "Too smart for your own good. Let's step outside."

Keith and Mike marched the Hardys toward an isolated exit. Along the way, Frank kept them talking. "So, I guess we know now why Tabitha made those large cash withdrawals."

"Our services don't come cheap," Mike said.

"Although we do enjoy our work," Keith said proudly.

"Like that little number you pulled in the subway?" Joe guessed.

Mike's smile was enough of an answer. "Sure," he said. "Not to mention the tape recorder. That was my idea actually. Too bad it didn't save us the trouble of wasting perfectly good bullets on you two."

"And the gas in the studio?" Frank said as they neared the exit. "Whose bright idea was that?"

"We came up with that one together," Keith said proudly. "Of course, we were really gunning for Randy."

"With Chang in prison, why did you guys still try to kill us?" Frank asked.

"We'd heard about you and were afraid you'd figure it out," Mike said. "Besides, you're punks."

"We weren't expecting Blue Lou to ante up," Keith said. "But it proved to be a great diversion. You dopes were being hit from both sides and never even knew it."

"It was easy for Tabitha to set up the murder," Frank said. "She knew Martinelli's whereabouts early in the game."

"Thanks to your brother." Mike laughed.

Frank and Joe stepped out of the exit into a dark passageway. A van was parked near the door.

"Move it," Mike said gruffly, prodding Frank in the back.

Joe wanted to make a grab at Keith, but he

reminded himself to remain cool. His opportunity would come, and he'd have to be ready.

Keith stepped in front of Joe, with the gun still leveled at him, and opened the side door of the van. That's when Joe got an even bigger shock. Randy Rand was in the back of the van, his hands tied behind his back, his mouth covered with a piece of duct tape.

"Get in," Mike commanded, jerking the gun in the direction of the van.

Frank and Joe slid in. Mike and Keith sat opposite them, their guns never wavering. Frank and Joe faced the front.

Joe heard the driver's door open. Tabitha Cowan climbed into the van, turned, and stared at the Hardys coldly.

"Tabitha," Joe said, disappointed. "I didn't want to believe you were responsible."

"Sorry to disappoint you," Tabitha said, "but you have to understand my side. Tight Fist Records is my last chance to prove to my father that I can be successful on my own. Counterfeiters like Martinelli were making it impossible for me to make a profit."

"So you had him killed," Frank said.

"It was like taking out the trash," Tabitha replied. "I hate what's going to happen to you, I really do. I had hoped that Mike and Keith could scare you away, but no such luck. Now I'm going to have to get rid of Randy, too."

Joe watched Randy's eyes widen above the black tape. He shook his head and started struggling against his bonds.

"What are you talking about?" Frank demanded.

"Randy's body will be found in an alley, shot," Tabitha said calmly. "Sorry, Randy, you'll be the random victim of a mugger. Poor Randy will die a tragic hero, and I'll make a fortune off his records," Tabitha went on smugly. "Of course, the two of you will be dumped in the East River. No ballads for Frank or Joe Hardy."

"You're insane," Joe muttered.

Tabitha glared at the Hardys. "Is it insane to want to live up to your father's expectations? To prove you have what it takes to carry on in his place someday? Tight Fist isn't the only thing on the line here. This is chump change compared to the inheritance I'll receive when my father dies."

"Sounds pretty warped to me," Frank said.

Tabitha threw her head back and laughed. "If it is, blame my father. He's the one who taught me everything I know. It's a dog-eat-dog world out there. It was either me or Martinelli. And it wasn't going to be me."

"What are you going to do, Tabitha?" Frank said, stalling for time. "Kill anyone who gets in your way? What about Blue Lou? What about the other counterfeiters who'll take his place while he's in jail?"

"I'll cross that bridge when I come to it," Tabitha said, putting her key into the ignition. "It's time for a ride. Your last one."

Joe stared at the gleeful expressions on Mike and Keith's faces. He nudged Frank with his knee, hoping he'd follow his lead. Simultaneously Frank and Joe lashed out with their feet, kicking the guns out of Mike and Keith's hands. Joe grabbed for Mike, administering several blows to the side of his head before he could react.

Joe was pleased to see that Frank had taken Keith out with a single old-fashioned roundhouse punch.

Joe glanced to the front. Tabitha stared in horror at them for one second before darting out of the van.

"She's getting away!" Joe shouted, sliding open the van door.

Then Joe got his last big shock of the night. Beastmaster J was standing in front of the van, holding on to Tabitha. He had pinned her arms to her sides. A line of security guards was now descending on the scene.

"I saw those guys leading you out of the back and thought something was up," the Beastmaster said.

Joe reached inside and untied Randy, who immediately leapt out of the van and shook the Beastmaster's hand.

"You're okay, man," Randy said. "You're really okay."

"Actually I just didn't want to get blamed for this, too," the Beastmaster said jokingly.

Joe and Frank stood nearby as the security team led Tabitha and her thugs away.

"You haven't seen the last of me," Tabitha swore, scowling as handcuffs were clamped to her wrists.

"Wow. And I used to like her," Joe said.

Frank and Joe stood near the stage as Randy went on, receiving thunderous applause. Beastmaster J stood next to them, watching Randy before his set.

"Now that Tabitha is safely locked away with Mike and Keith, we can finally enjoy ourselves," Joe said.

"We did well," Frank agreed. "We put away three killers and a major mob counterfeiter in the same weekend. "It's definitely time for some R and R."

"Luckily, Randy's had three offers of new labels," Joe said, "all in the last ten minutes."

"Pedro Torres says he thinks he can bust Chang's operation with what he found in the warehouse," Frank reminded his brother.

Joe watched Randy perform and grinned. "I'm just glad Mike and Keith are willing to testify against Tabitha. She sure turned out to be more than a shrewd businesswoman."

"That's for sure," Frank shouted over the screaming crowd.

"I guess the police tests will tell if one of those guns Mike and Steve were carrying was the murder weapon," Joe said, glancing out at the stage. A huge wave of fans was pressing the stage security back and working its way onto the stage as Randy grabbed his mike and burst into "What U Do."

"Come on," Joe said to Frank. "We'd better give them a hand."

Frank and Joe rushed onstage to help hold the fans back. Screaming, wide-eyed girls clutched at Frank. He detoured them as gently as possible until security reinforcements came in.

"How would you like to do that for a living?" Joe shouted into Frank's ear as they went backstage, where Beastmaster J was still lingering.

"No thanks," Frank replied.

After the music stopped, Randy stepped up in front of the Power Brokers. "Before I continue," he said to the packed arena, "I want to make a public apology to Beastmaster J for the song I wrote about him and the way I've been dissing him and his music. He's a great person and terrific artist, and I want him to join me out here for a new song."

Beastmaster J acted shocked.

"Go ahead," Joe prodded him.

The Beastmaster stepped out on the stage, the crowd howling their approval. He and Randy shook hands.

"There are two other dudes I want to thank for getting me out of a huge mess recently. If you're ever in a jam, these are the dudes to call."

Randy nodded at the Power Brokers and they began to play. Frank stared, astonished, as Randy sang, the Beastmaster joining him on the chorus:

"Yo, it's Frank and Joe / Yo, it's Frank and Joe / if you're innocent of the crime / if you're staring at hard time / if the walls are closing in / if your options are running thin / Yo, it's Frank and Joe / Yo, it's Frank and Joe / Frank and Joe will come through / Frank and Joe know what to do / don't even think about making tracks / just fill these homeys in on the facts / Yo, it's Frank and Joe / Yo, it's Frank and Joe . . ."

"I bet it'll be a hit," Joe said with a big grin.

"It's definitely fresh," Frank agreed.

Frank and Joe's next case:

The Hardys are working on a high-risk, high-stakes undercover operation. A hijacking ring is spreading terror through New York, snatching high-priced cars at gunpoint. Posing as expert thieves, Frank and Joe follow the gang from the streets of the city to the islands of the Caribbean—into the heart of an international black-marketing scheme!

But down in the islands, it's open season on the brothers. Cut off from the outside world and from outside help, they discover that their cover has been blown. They're driving a dangerous road—hard and fast and slick—and one slip of the wheel could lead to a deadly end. But when Frank and Joe get in gear, there's no turning back . . . in *Road Pirates,* Case #74 in The Hardy Boys Casefiles™.